A Candlelight Ecstasy Romance®

FOR A SUSPENDED MOMENT, THEIR GAZES HELD. . . .

The ropes and the wicker of the balloon's gondola creaked like a ship asea. Unseen insects whirred and droned. Leaves rustled in the wind. The wild beat of Loy's heart deafened her to them all.

She suddenly realized his full weight pressed upon her. Her breasts were flattened against his chest; her legs were tangled with his as only a lover's should be. His silver buckle bit into the softness of her stomach; his blue jeans scratched the length of her bare legs. But Loy didn't notice her discomfort. She was aware of one thing only: his mouth poised a breath away from her own. . . .

A CANDLELIGHT ECSTASY ROMANCE ®

CHAMPAGNE FLIGHT

Prudence Martin

A CANDLELIGHT ECSTASY ROMANCE ®

Published by
Dell Publishing Co., Inc.
1 Dag Hammarskjold Plaza
New York, New York 10017

Dell ® TM 681510, Dell Publishing Co., Inc.
Candlelight Ecstasy Romance®, 1,203,540, is a registered
trademark of Dell Publishing Co., Inc.,
New York, New York.

ISBN: 0-440-12041-1

Printed in the United States of America
First printing—August 1983

*With special thanks to
those aeronauts extraordinaire,
Ray and Cathy DiTirro.
May your Rainbow always soar
high amidst the clouds.*

To Our Readers:

We have been delighted with your enthusiastic response to Candlelight Ecstasy Romances®, and we thank you for the interest you have shown in this exciting series.

In the upcoming months we will continue to present the distinctive, sensuous love stories you have come to expect only from Ecstasy. We look forward to bringing you many more books from your favorite authors and also the very finest work from new authors of contemporary romantic fiction.

As always we are striving to present the unique, absorbing love stories that you enjoy most—books that are more than ordinary romance. Your suggestions and comments are always welcome. Please write to us at the address below.

Sincerely,

The Editors
Candlelight Romances
1 Dag Hammarskjold Plaza
New York, New York 10017

CHAPTER ONE

The realization that she was being watched crept up on Loy McDaniel gradually. It began with a prickling along her spine as she bent over the edge of the trailer to retrieve her pilot's log. She straightened slowly. As the sensation subsided she grimaced wryly, a self-conscious denial of her foolish jitters.

She collected her log and turned. The hairs on the back of her neck stood straight up. Loy resisted the incredible urge to run. Flicking back unruly ripples of flaxen hair, she surreptitiously glanced around.

Heated shafts of late afternoon sun lanced the ever-changing motley collection of pilots conferring with passengers and excited onlookers. Her eyes swept past a whiskered gentleman, in full military regalia topped by a leather aviator's cap, exchanging views with a lanky youth wearing only bright orange tennis shorts. Beyond them she could see several children romping on a strip of mowed grass bordering the cement lot. Slouching against bumpers or loitering in trailers, crews casually swapped tales over cans of beer. No one appeared the least interested in the owner of Cloud Sailing, Inc.

Loy shrugged. A too-active imagination, most likely generated from lack of sleep the previous night. Stretching her long, deeply tanned legs before her, she leaned against the trailer and flipped open her log. She checked the silver watch gracing her narrow wrist, then reached to tap against the back window of her red-striped Scout. Suddenly she froze. Tiny, tingling bumps rose along her arms. Snapping the log shut, she swung her head around, eyes anxiously searching the crowds shifting between the multitude of four-wheel drives and station wagons dotted over the parking lot. After a minute the goose bumps faded.

Paranoia, she laughed to herself. She took a step toward the Scout.

And then she saw him.

He stood beside a placard reading BALLOONISTS GET IT UP WITH HOT AIR, a tall, browned figure in faded jeans and navy blue T-shirt. She couldn't see his face. It was obscured by a camera aimed directly at her. In dawning outrage Loy realized he was snapping shot after shot of her and had been for some time. God knew how long he'd been surveying her, taking pictures of her and all the while she'd been unaware of being caught on film.

It made her feel utterly vulnerable. And vulnerable was the one thing Loy had vowed never to be again.

She whirled around, marching purposefully to the other side of the vehicle. Once she was out of the stranger's view, she relaxed slightly, reminding herself it was nothing unusual. Wherever there was a balloon rally there was certain to be a dozen or so camera addicts snapping away. Even as she told herself this, Loy looked over her shoulder to make certain she was no longer the focus of anyone's lens.

Not that she would have minded being the subject, had she known about it beforehand. Loy wasn't overly conceited about her looks, but she knew men were often attracted to her features. To her own eyes, her angular face was marred by a wide brow, high cheekbones, and a lower lip that was definitely too full. Her nose was long and narrow and dusted with detested freckles. She privately considered her oval, beryl blue eyes to be her greatest asset, but generally Loy didn't give her looks much thought.

Now she reflected that she wouldn't have minded posing for the unknown photographer if he'd asked. It was

10

being caught off guard that annoyed her. It set her at a disadvantage.

Sighing, Loy pushed the incident out of her mind. She wouldn't let it ruin her evening. She slapped her log book against the Scout's window, attracting Gary's attention as he sprawled in the front seat.

"It's getting close to six," she said, holding up her wrist to indicate the time. "Are you sure this charter you arranged knew where he was to meet us?"

"Sure. He even said he'd probably be early."

"Well, if he doesn't show up soon, we'll just go up without him," said Loy, tossing her log into his lap.

He caught it easily, then grinned. "You mean if we ever get past debating about where to launch."

"Oh, we'll launch eventually; we always do," she said as she slipped away. She worked her way through the fluctuating sea of people, stopping occasionally to exchange greetings with friends or to pass on bits of advice or encouragement to newcomers. She paused to joke with the crew lounging in the back of Bob Coulter's trailer about the perpetual round of conferences preceding any multiple launching. Her laughter stopped abruptly as she heard the unmistakable click of a camera.

Spinning, she saw him standing less than twelve feet away. He continued to snap, the automatic wind on his camera eliminating the need for him to pause between shots. A sudden, senseless fury exploded within Loy. She stalked back to her Scout and leaped nimbly into the driver's seat beside a surprised Gary. With a short, angry jerk she thrust into gear and shot out of the lot. As she passed Coulter's crew she glimpsed the cameraman lowering his equipment. She chose to ignore his dazzling flash of white teeth.

"I take it you've decided on a launch site," said Gary in dry observation.

"They'll dither all night about where to go, when to go," she muttered. Then, glancing at him, her ill-humor

11

vanished as instantly as it had appeared. The knowing look in his eyes made her sigh at her own impulsiveness. "I just can't stand all this waiting around while every possible target angle is dissected. What is it about ballooning that makes for so much discussion? We do more talking than we ever do flying, that's for damn sure!"

"Where do you think we get all the hot air?" he asked in deliberately mild tones.

Loy laughed. Gary Schaeffer's tranquil attitude always had a calming effect on her. He was rather like an overstuffed teddy bear come to life, as broad as he was tall, with a gentle nature that belied his large frame. He wasn't easily rattled by her quick temper, nor was he the least threatening to her sexually. He was the one man around whom Loy felt totally comfortable.

As they drove off, several other vehicles pulled out behind them filled with eager balloonists who were glad to be going anywhere, doing anything, rather than simply waiting around. They wound through a suburban neighborhood, passing kids on bikes and barking dogs, then turned a corner and abruptly found themselves in one of the patches of rural countryside on the fringes of metropolitan Kansas City.

Lushly leafed trees fenced the twisting road, parting occasionally to present a view of patioed backyards, paved streets, or small, empty fields. The warm spring sun hovered in the west, sneaking through the trees to speckle the road. Loy and Gary scanned the surrounding landscape for a suitable launching site, searching for an unobstructed field at least five miles in the necessary wind direction from the target.

"See anything?" Loy called out the window to the two teenagers riding in the trailer.

"Not yet!" yelled Roger.

Through her side mirror she could see the pair standing beside the covered gondola, each gripping the trailer railing with one hand while holding a can of cola with the other. Scruffy manes of dark hair tossed in the wind; tall, gangly bodies jounced in unison. The Perren brothers were young but hardworking and reliable crew members. Loy returned her eyes to the road, thinking this would be a good summer for Cloud Sailing.

"So what happened back there?" inquired Gary after a long silence.

"What makes you think something happened?" she returned.

He grinned, lifted a can of beer to his lips. "You were shooting more sparks than a firecracker on the Fourth of July." He sipped and waited.

Splashes of white orchids over maroon cotton shifted as Loy shrugged her shoulders. Gary was a good friend, one of the few people she let get close to her, but not even to him could she explain her intense sensitivity to another's control. He wouldn't understand her feeling of defenseless exposure, her impotent anger at being caught unaware by the unknown photographer. She needed to make her own choices, her own mistakes; to have someone else choosing for her undermined her hard-gained independence.

"How about over there?" she said, pointing a long finger toward an open field. An iron chain blocked the property and a small sign read NO TRESPASSING.

Gary examined it. "Looks pretty good. Hang on."

He lumbered out of the vehicle, lifting himself over the chain. He paced back and forth, surveying, then returned to squint his puppy-brown eyes up at Loy's window. "The ground looks pretty good. I think I can remove the chain."

"Just hold it down and I'll drive over it."

As Gary placed his weight against the length of iron links, pinning it to the ground, Loy drove bumpily over it and onto the field. The small caravan of balloonists crossed the field behind her, vehicles jolting over ruts and crew members hanging on to gondolas and trailers to keep from being bounced loose. By the time Loy had reversed her car and parked facing the evening wind, Gary had loped across to meet her.

Together they moved to the back where Roger and his younger brother, Danny, were already hauling out the envelope bag. As they opened it and began towing the balloon out over the field, Loy and Gary uncovered and dragged the gondola out of the trailer. With practiced efficiency they quickly attached uprights, inserted instruments and burner, then tipped the wicker basket over on its side in front of where the balloon had been spread out. Dozens of color-coded cables were unraveled to connect the envelope to the gondola. Loy turned to bring the motorized blower fan forward.

She plowed directly into firm male musculature. "Oh! Excuse—" she began, then choked.

The identifying Nikon slung over his shoulder wasn't needed to tell Loy who this was. The instant jangling along her nerve endings had told her it was her shutterbug. Every protective instinct she possessed warned her to have nothing to do with him.

"Do you always lead your parade onto private property?" he inquired in a pleasantly low voice.

Her mouth actually opened as Loy prepared to explain that this "private property" was owned by the amusement park over which they were to fly, the park which fully sanctioned this rally. But in that same flitting instant, indignation bubbled up and Loy shut it again. Why should she tell him anything? She didn't owe him explanations!

She stepped to the side, then halted as he moved to block her. "Will you excuse me?" she snapped without looking at him.

"No," he replied easily.

Her head whipped up at that and she gazed directly into a pair of flecked green eyes that sparkled with amusement behind a thick fringe of dark lashes. Lines crinkled the outer corners, radiating a humor that annoyed Loy. She pulled her eyes away from his. Fixing her gaze coldly on

14

his camera equipment, she said in tones brimming with hostility, "Whatever your game is, I don't have time to play it."

"I'm not playing games," he returned. His voice rustled with unspoken meaning. "Just give me your name and phone number and I'll step out of the way."

That brought her gaze swinging back to his. This time she really took note of the man. Hair the color of sun-warmed sand layered in soft contrast to the hard structure of his face. The squared jawline spoke of strength, yet the features erased any hint of harshness. The slender nose tilted at the tip and the narrow lips lifted in a self-assured grin. Deep dimples dented both sides of an altogether extremely handsome face.

For several seconds Loy could do no more than stand and stare. Then she relaxed slightly. She knew how to deal with egotistical wolves. Setting her hands on the waist-band of her khaki hiking shorts, she directed a gelid glare at him. "I don't think you heard me. I don't have time for indulging in flirtations. We're trying to get a balloon up, in case you hadn't noticed."

"Oh, I noticed," he said, not the least disconcerted by either her damping tones or her discouraging words. "That's why I'm certain you'll want to give me your name and number as quickly as possible."

What Loy wanted to give him was a slap in the face. She certainly didn't intend to give him anything else. She pivoted on her heel, planning to go around the other side of the basket. His hand grasped her arm, riveting her in place. She stared in disbelief at the long fingers coiled around her arm. Who on earth did this man think he was?

She was about to wrench her arm free when he dropped it. At the same instant she felt a reassuring hand cloak her shoulder.

"Anything here I can help you with?" Gary politely inquired of the stranger.

There were definite advantages to having a friend the

15

size of a toolshed—and as well equipped, thought Loy as she looked at Gary's massive hand protectively curling on her upper arm. The smile she presented the shutterbug was almost smug.

He looked more amused than abashed, thereby irritating her further. His disturbing gaze lingered on her one long moment, telling her plainly he wasn't through with her, before shifting to meet Gary's brown eyes. He extended his hand. His smile was friendly, confident, and, to Loy's eyes, detestably charming.

"You must be Loy McDaniel," he said, startling them both. "I've chartered you to take me up tonight. I'm Derett Graham."

"You!" squeaked Loy while Gary grinned broadly and shook his head. He firmly grasped the proffered hand.

"You're mistaken. My name's Gary Schaeffer, crew chief for Cloud Sailing."

Puzzlement flicked through Derett Graham's eyes. He glanced toward Roger and Danny and past them. "Then where is McDaniel?" he asked, his eyes still searching the field.

Not only a wolf with an oversized ego, but a chauvinist too! Loy drew herself up to her full five foot six inches and shrugged free of Gary's arm. Looking up to glare directly at him, she said with ringing disdain, "*I'm* Loy McDaniel, Mr. Graham. I am the owner of Cloud Sailing and I will be your pilot tonight."

"You!" he said in a deeper imitation of her earlier surprise. His gaze ran from the top of her wheaten tresses to the bottom of her Adidas-clad toes. She had the feeling he now took exception to the curves outlined in maroon cotton and tan khaki, a feeling justified by his statement of incredulity. "*You're* the balloon pilot?"

Although his attitude annoyed her, Loy experienced an immense satisfaction in being able to burst some of his complacency. Her lips curved in an unfriendly smile.

16

"*Owner* and pilot. But I won't be the pilot of anything tonight if we don't stop wasting time."

All around them spattered daubs of flattened fabric were struggling to rise, spangling the sky with a spectrum of brilliant hues. Graham stepped aside and Loy, together with Gary, at last hauled the blower fan into place before their unfurled balloon. The two teens held the skirt of the envelope open while Gary anchored the crown with a tether rope. Cottonball puffs of clouds brushing past a stylized ring of treetops began taking shape on the sky-blue teardrop balloon as it filled with air. Loy knelt within the tipped-over basket and blasted the burner on. As the inflated balloon stretched upward, she righted the basket and issued a terse command to Derett to get in.

He did so with agility, flinging his long legs over the brown suede rim of the basket. Other balloons were lifting in resplendent splashes of color. The crew walked the balloon to a slice of free space and let go. They slowly sailed into a startling sky of azure whisped with white. Loy busied herself with maneuvering, engineering their ascent with well-timed bursts of heat from the burner. The sound overwhelmed the small basket, making conversation impossible.

Then they were gliding with the wind into the flamboyant mosaic checkering the sky. Derett aimed his camera at the diminishing wavers below, then at the rainbow of balloons surrounding them. Most bore vividly colorful patterns. Some displayed well-known product labels, others spectacular individual designs. To one side of them drifted a droll reproduction of a gumball machine, to the other, a fabulous fanning of a peacock's iridescent tail. Loy watched her passenger slowly rotating to capture them all. As he came round to face her, he lowered his camera and pursed his lips in a silent whistle.

"So the lady really is a pilot."

She leaned on the edge of the wicker and surveyed the

landscape, ignoring him. She hadn't been paid to take his insults.

"Is this a race?" he asked.

She hit the blast valve, sending propane heat into the envelope and deafening them with a hissing whoosh.

"Is this a race?" he asked again as the sound faded.

Loy permitted herself a glance at him. He was smiling, indenting his cheeks with those incredibly deep dimples. He looked warmly congenial. And unbelievably appealing. She felt her animosity slipping away. She wanted to grasp at it, to hug her enmity to her bosom like some talisman against evil. But his engaging grin and sparkling eyes were proving to be too powerfully attractive.

"No," she answered reluctantly, her eyes sliding past his shoulder. "There's really no such thing as a balloon race, since we can't control wind speed or horizontal direction. Balloon races are actually tests of skill and accuracy. Right now, we're flying in what's known as CNT."

His sandy brows raised and she noticed that the left one was spliced by a tiny white scar. She pointed to a well-mown grassy field beyond the amusement park. "Convergent Navigational Task. We fly in toward a specific goal. Our target's over there. Whoever lands closest to the target is the 'winner.'"

"What do you win?"

"For this, nothing. This is just for fun and good will. But at recognized races"—she paused to hit the burner, taking them up over a border of trees—"you sometimes get money, sometimes points toward the Nationals."

The breeze playfully whisked a long strand of light amber hair across her face. Before she pulled it back into place he snapped a picture of her. She frowned. "I wish you wouldn't do that."

"What are the Nationals?" he inquired, brushing off her comment as if her wishes were scarcely important.

She bit back her annoyance. "The U.S. National Championship Competition. Held in Indianola, Iowa, each year at the end of July."

They floated over the park, where lush landscaping was interspersed with looped roller coasters, paddlewheelers, Ferris wheels, and other rides. On the paved streets people stopped and pointed upward. They could hear the exclamations, the shouted greetings, and the distant discharge from other burners. A train whistle blew and arms waved from windows as passengers helloed. The clicking of Derett's camera was non-stop. His stance stiffened almost imperceptibly each time, followed by a fleeting relaxation. The muscles beneath the navy T-shirt shifted accordingly. When Loy realized she was staring at the flexure of his body, she hit the burner hard and sent them up with a slight swaying.

He turned, raising his brows. His light brown hair ruffled gently, then the wind caught hold of the basket in a seemingly motionless movement. "I can't believe how still this is. We hardly seem to be moving at all and yet we're cruising past all this scenery." He flung out an arm for emphasis.

She stared at the glint of sunlight on the tawny hair dusting his arms, then determinedly fixed her eyes on the leather thong that held the small storage compartment closed. She released the thong and the wooden door dropped. As she pulled out a small stack of business cards she said coolly, "The wind holds us still. Is this your first ride?"

"Yes," he replied. He cast his eyes over the verdant park below and the kaleidoscopic array of balloons around them. He brought his gaze back to her face. "But not, I'm sure, my last."

His tone rippled with intimations Loy preferred to ignore. She began casually tossing her cards into the air, watching them drift lazily down to the crowds.

"May I?" Derett put out his hand and without thinking Loy handed him a card. Though she'd held it by the very

19

edge, their fingers met. She jerked back as if bitten by an adder. Their eyes locked, then she focused upward as she took refuge in the din of the burner. Out of the corner of her eye she watched him peruse her card. She caught the flicker of surprise and knew he'd read the line, Flight Instruction. My God, the man was a chauvinist of the highest order!

"You do promotions, sales, and instruction in addition to charters?" he asked with an amazement that confirmed her opinion of him.

"Yes," she replied tersely.

"I thought this might be a hobby—or a second income," he quickly amended at the daggered glower she threw his way.

"Well, it isn't. It's my business. And please spare me your surprise over a *woman* being in this kind of business!" she added with unnecessary force.

He laughed. Loy's nerves gave an involuntary leap through her system at the melodious resonance. Her eyes followed the motion of his hand as he tucked the card into the back pocket of his jeans. She noted the lean lines of his hip, the solid thews of his thighs and instantly chided herself for doing so. She didn't want to notice *anything* about him! The absolute last thing she wanted in her life was another man to mess it up.

She presented him with her profile, determined not to so much as glance at him again. She heard his shutter release snap and swiveled her head to find his lens pointed at her.

"Please, don't do that," she said sharply.

"Why not? You're a lovely subject." He tipped his head to the side, his hair brushing against the tanned column of his neck. He studied her soberly, as though viewing a painting or some other inanimate object. "With your heart-shaped face, delicate features, and wildly waving hair—is that natural?" At her nod, he continued. "You look like a pre-Raphaelite beauty."

20

"Whatever sort of *beauty*"—she infused the word with scorn—"you may think I am, it doesn't give you the right to take pictures of me without my consent."

If she'd hoped to discomfit him, she failed. He smiled at her, clearly unperturbed, and said, "In the future I promise to ask permission first."

She did not deign to tell him there would be no *future* for them. But her expression must have spoken for her because he chuckled a low, teasing laugh that stroked her every cell. Stretching out a fingertip, Derett lightly traced the outline of an orchid over the shoulder of her blouse. His touch burned through the thin cotton, branding her. Though her nerves shrieked, Loy felt too mesmerized to protest. Abruptly he shifted his stance. His thigh was a whisper away from hers. She found herself staring in fascination at the faded denim stretched tautly over his leg.

"I could look forward to a future with you, Loy McDaniel," he said softly.

Her head jerked up. His breath caressed her cheek. Her heart ricocheted against her rib cage. His soughing "May I?" brushed her lips. Then he leaned back, braced himself, and took another photo of her. Loy almost snarled in outrage.

They floated wordlessly over an audience filling an amphitheater, then began lowering as they passed the outer edge of the amusement park. Balloons were touching down all around them and Loy's skill as a pilot was evidenced by her ability to judge the path of the wind current necessary to avoid ramming into another balloon. As they neared the grass she ordered briskly, "Squat back, but don't sit, as soon as we touch down. With only two of us, this might be a little bumpy, but don't worry. I have it under control." The last challenged him to deny it. He didn't.

The gondola was dragged several feet along the field, jarring them until finally rocking to a halt. On the roadway several cars were stopped as spectators gathered to watch this showy mass descent. Chase vehicles were driving onto the grass and even as Loy and Derett righted, they could see her crew barreling toward them.

She threw her long legs over the basket's edge. Derett's hand instantly shot out to steady her. Quivers sprinted from her elbow up her arm. With an impatient scowl Loy yanked free of his unwanted assistance. Did he think she was helpless?

"Don't get out until I tell you to," she said to him in a curt directive.

"Aye, aye, cap'n," he said, proffering a cheerful salute.

She gnashed her teeth but said nothing. *Let him mock, if he wants to,* she thought angrily. After tonight she'd never see him again! As Gary, Roger, and Danny tumbled from the Scout to begin deflating the balloon with coordinated efficiency, she grabbed her log and quickly noted the flight times. Then she signaled to Graham who climbed from the basket with lithe grace.

Air was pressed out of the flattened envelope. The lines were bound together with colored tape and unhooked and the fabric was rolled into the bag. The gondola top was taken off and the instrument panel was removed. Within minutes everything was returned to the trailer.

Loy overheard Derett's pleasant tones as she went back to the ice chest stored in the Scout. She told herself she wasn't straining to hear him ask of Gary, "How did you get into ballooning? Have you been in it long?"

"I've been in it a little over a year," replied Gary. "Loy decided I should become part of Cloud Sailing—and her decisions are instant and irrevocable. She's been in the business for a little over two years, though she's been ballooning for nearly five."

She rattled around in the ice, freeing an embedded bottle of California champagne, and missed the next comments. But as she straightened with the bottle in hand she clearly heard Graham's voice from the other side of the Scout.

"Well, it's not exactly my idea of a womanly pursuit, but she handled it okay."

Fury nearly strangled her. How dare he! His idea of a womanly pursuit indeed! Handled it okay? She was a damn good pilot—one of the best in the area! Loy had no clear notions what she wanted to do, but throttling Derett Graham and his condescending chauvinist attitudes was paramount among them. As she stood shaking with wrath, she realized she was shaking the champagne. And with the realization came a gradual smile of saccharine sweetness.

After ripping the gold foil from the top, she did an impromptu imitation of the rumba with the bottle serving as her maraca. Then she swiftly strode to where her crew and Derett leaned against the front of the Scout. She held the champagne up and saw appreciation flash through Derett's glittering green eyes.

"To celebrate your initiation in lighter-than-air flight," she said in a voice dripping syrup. Her fingers pulled the wire from the cork, and as it popped into the air, she added, "It's traditional."

A foaming, fizzing spray doused Derett. Loy aimed the bottle up, then down, drenching his hair, shirt, and jeans. A stunned silence from her crew had instantaneously given way to chortles at Derett's obvious shock. The darkening sea blue of Loy's eyes warned the three not to say a word about the traditional mere dribbling upon the head. Even as she glanced from them to Derett he was recovering.

He joined in their laughter, seeming to enjoy the joke at his expense. And even through her pleasure at having disconcerted him, Loy felt an unwilling admiration. It had been a long time since she'd known a man who could laugh at himself.

CHAPTER TWO

It wasn't until the phone rang at ten o'clock that Loy realized she'd given Derett Graham her number. It was listed directly below her name on her card. *Drat and damn,* she thought as she slapped her novel shut. She unfolded her slender figure from the depths of her favorite chair and rose to cross the room.

The shaggy gray and white rug at her feet stirred, then bounded against Loy's bare knees with a buoyant bark that drowned out the ringing. She bumped into the end table and reached for the phone with a shaking hand.

"Hello?" Surely her breathlessness was due to the dog's antics and not to any unwarranted anticipation on her part.

"Loy, what's wrong? Why's Jeeves barking like that?"

She couldn't understand her plunging disappointment. She didn't *want* Derett to call her, did she? She should be relieved!

"Shush, Jeeves! Down, down!" She thrust the Old English sheepdog away from her legs. "Nothing's wrong, Keith. You know Jeeves. What's up?"

"I think I've got a charter for you, babe. A biggie," said Keith in his typical slow rumble.

"Hang on, will you?" said Loy. She set down the receiver and collared Jeeves, who seemed to think the object of this new game was to knock Loy down as often as possible. Muttering dire threats about obedience school, she finally managed to shove him out of her living room and into an

24

expansive fenced yard. When she came back to pick up the phone, she could hear Keith whistling off-key. Funny how that whistle sounded fine, even welcome, to her now. When they were married it had driven her crazy.

"What's this about a charter?" she asked, cutting into a warbling rendition of *You Are My Sunshine*.

"Well, it's nothing certain, babe, but if it comes off, it could mean some big bucks."

She counted to three. "If *what* comes off, Keith?"

"The *NewSports* charter."

"Keith, if you don't explain what all this is about, I'm going to—"

"Okay, okay. *NewSports* magazine called the club," he said, referring to the exclusive athletic club he managed. Loy knew he often got such calls from various people wanting inside information about offbeat sports. Keith Brenner's reputation as a sports enthusiast and general man-in-the-know had spread beyond local boundaries. "They wanted to know of a balloonist willing to train a journalist in piloting. They plan to send the journalist to cover the Nationals from the 'ground up,' so to speak."

Loy coiled the phone cord around her index finger. "Why wouldn't they just send a journalist up with a balloonist?"

"Hey, babe, you know me—"

She did, all too well.

"I don't ask why. But I wanted you to know I gave 'em your name so you can expect to hear from 'em in a couple days."

"Thanks, Keith. A lot." She let her finger slip free of the cord and added with genuine warmth, "You know I appreciate it whenever you send someone my way.

"I still look out for my own, doll. Jackie sends her best."

Accepting his wife's best and returning it, Loy promised to let Keith know when *NewSports* had called. She hung up, then stood motionless, her gaze fixed unseeingly on the cinnamon chenille of the couch.

His own. After nearly three years he still thought he had to look out after her. Keith had always striven to protect her. Too much so. He'd treated her like a helpless doll, nearly smothering her during the five years of their marriage. But he'd cared for her, protected her, loved her. With a drawn-out sigh that seemed to hang in the air, she closed her eyes and wondered for the millionth time why she hadn't made her marriage to Keith work. He was such a nice guy. If she couldn't make a go of it with him, she couldn't make a go of it, period.

An unaccustomed self-pity settled over Loy. She wasn't one to waste time feeling sorry for herself or being depressed, but tonight she felt oddly out of sorts. She should be jubilant. Big bucks, Keith had said. Lord knew she could use some big bucks. She tried to focus on the prospect of hearing from *NewSports.* Instead, an image rose before her of dimples that indented boyishly beside a mouth that slid slowly into a smile, of warm green eyes flecked with brown beneath uneven sandy brows.

Her eyes flew open. It irritated Loy to remember what Derett Graham's mouth did. Worse, it frightened her to remember how her skin had tingled beneath the heated survey of his eyes. She didn't trust those tingles, not one bit. Those were the kind of tingles that led to trouble with a capital T. Hadn't she already painfully learned that—twice?

She looked around at the eclectic furnishings that her sister Lisle termed twentieth-century attic. The pottery lamps on matching walnut-grain tables at either end of the couch. The oak ladderback rocker angled for ease in watching the portable television set in the opposite corner. The tiered plant stand in front of the double window. The lumpy, faded floral armchair that she'd had since the early days of her marriage. Her first marriage, that is.

Of course, *that* marriage had been an understandable mistake. She'd been so young—and so foolish, thought Loy now. She'd met Stan Herndon at the campaign headquarters for a district candidate where she'd gotten a summer job after graduating from high school. She was the office gofer. He was the youth coordinator. To Loy he was the epitome of well-dressed success. He was the Vietnam veteran with long-term political ambitions that awed her. He was the older man with extensive knowledge of the world. He was the president of his college class who could bring a crowd to a roar with his speeches and reduce her to putty with his whispers. He was the workaholic who finished a four-year course in three years. Not without her help, however, she bitterly reminded herself.

Casting her slim frame into the corner of the couch, Loy thought about the summer day, nearly ten years ago, when she'd married Stan Herndon against her parents' advice, then about the years that followed. While Stan threw himself into an overload of classes the fall after their wedding, Loy diligently went to work to support them. She worked as a low-paid clerk at the college during the day and waitressed at night. Though Stan swore it would be only for the semester, it turned out to be for the next and the next and the next after that.

It was, in fact, the pattern for the whole of their marriage. They scarcely saw each other. And with each course Stan completed, his wife's high school opinions meant less and less. They ceased conversing; when they talked at all, Stan talked to Loy in the tones of an instructor with a particularly slow pupil. He constantly exhorted her to "improve" herself. Her clothes, her hair, her speech, her posture—*everything* had to be bettered to pass muster as a future political wife. Their lovemaking faded into nothingness. It seemed they were too busy or too tired for it the entire last year of their marriage. Of course, any question of children was thoroughly squashed by Stan, who insisted they wait until he finished law school. A rising politician couldn't be burdened with a family, after all.

When a "kind friend" told Loy about Stan's "other woman," she was almost relieved. For the first time in three years she made a decision of her own. As Stan headed for law school Loy headed for divorce court.

The worst bruising had been to her ego, Loy knew that now. But at the time, her wound was fresh and agonizing. At twenty-one, she hadn't realized that time would salve her hurt. She thought everyone must be laughing at gullible Loy who'd worked her buns off to support her husband's mistress. In her embarrassment, in her need to feel secure and accepted by someone, in her desire to "show them," she'd made her unforgivable mistake. Her second marriage.

She could forgive her young and foolish heart in falling for Stan Herndon's charming address, but Loy found it hard to excuse having taken advantage of Keith Brenner's loving kindness.

She'd taken a hop, skip, and jump from Stan's loveless arms to Keith Brenner's muscled hammerlock. There couldn't be a man less like Stan Herndon alive. In contrast to Stan's lithe, medium, ever-polished figure, Keith was a broad, firmly muscled, casual athlete. Instead of being a fiery orator, he rarely spoke, content to listen to Loy, who found it thrilling to be listened to for a change. He never read anything that wasn't related to sports statistics and he had no desire to make the world sit up and notice him. Appearances meant nothing to Keith. All he wanted from Loy was to take care of her.

She'd met him at the diner where she waitressed. Every night he'd come in and order a brownie with a scoop of ice cream. He'd eat it slowly, watching her every move with his soulful eyes. He'd eat and watch and listen to her pour out her troubles. His kind, stolid presence was a comforting mainstay to her when her marriage to Stan broke down. The night she told him she'd filed for divorce Keith pushed his brownie to the side, leaned over the counter, and proposed. And he made it clear from the start that no wife of his was ever going to work. His woman, he pronounced sternly, would stay at home like a woman should. After three years of juggling a marathon of jobs, it sounded like heaven to Loy.

She knew she didn't love Keith, but she told herself love would come. He was kind and good and he loved her. She was certain she would learn to love him. Three weeks after her divorce from Stan was finalized, she became Mrs. Keith Brenner.

It came as a shock to discover that she was not Keith's biggest passion. Football, baseball, hockey, racing, boxing, even Ping-Pong roused him in ways she never could. He was the ultimate sportsman. From the moment he awoke to the moment he went to sleep, he breathed sports. She came in second—a protected and loved second, but that wasn't satisfactory to Loy's emotional needs. By their first anniversary Loy knew she would never, could never, love Keith. But she was determined to make this marriage work, regardless of love.

Loy put off having children, hoping Keith would grow up, would tire of eternally playing games. But he didn't. He remained a sweet, overgrown boy, moving from tennis to squash, from skiing to snowmobiling. And all the while he swaddled her in an overprotective cocoon that reduced her to feeling like a fragile piece of porcelain. She wanted to feel like a person, to be recognized as a capable, thinking human being.

By the time Keith got into ballooning, they both knew their relationship was floundering. In a last effort to save their marriage, Loy immersed herself in ballooning, accompanying him on flights, working as his crew, chasing after him in their beat-up sedan. She even got her FAA pilot's license for lighter-than-air craft. But they continued to drift apart. One day she'd simply told Keith she thought they should call it quits. He'd stared at her steadily for several seconds, then mildly agreed. There had been no arguing, no animosity.

Loy ended up with the house, the dog, and the ballooning equipment—along with the equipment payments. Desperate for money, Loy ventured into the aviation business. With the help of Lisle, who took calls and scheduled flights, and Keith, who referred interested club members to her, she began taking charters in the evenings and on weekends while holding a nine-to-five secretarial position for one of Kansas City's leading accounting firms. It was there that she'd learned how to handle the necessary business paperwork. Eventually her charter business made enough for her to expand into equipment sales and training. She'd left the accounting firm last spring. The same week Keith's wife, Jackie, gave birth to their son.

Clicking her tongue against her teeth, Loy jumped up from the chair. What was the sense in going over all her past failures? She didn't need to remind herself that she was a jinx at love. Her fulfillment didn't need to come from a man. She had her business. She lived her own life, made her own decisions. She was an independent person!

"And that," she declared in a furious whisper as she went to call Jeeves in, "is just the way I like it!"

But as she crawled into bed Loy recalled teasing laughter and pleasant masculine tones, a scorching touch and a searing glance. And she fell asleep yearning for something she knew she could never have.

The first bottle arrived at nine. Loy stared blankly at the champagne the young man had handed her. Dom Pérignon!

"There must be some mistake," she said. "I didn't order —"

"It's prepaid, ma'am," interjected the cheery youth helpfully as he backed away from her front door.

"But this is much too expensive! Who—?" she began, only to find that the delivery van was pulling out of her driveway. A square white card dangled from a crimson ribbon around the bottle's golden neck. She hesitated, uncertain as to why. In a spurt of self-anger, she flipped it over.

Save this for our next flight . . .

No signature. She didn't recognize the handwriting, which was a bold block print. A sudden shiver raced from her fingertips to her toes. A vision of glittering eyes, tilting lips, and deep dimples flashed in her mind. Holding the champagne at arm's length, she eyed it with the look of one confronting an alien beast.

Derett Graham obviously thought a lot of himself. Well, this champagne would turn to vinegar before she took him up for another flight!

She smacked shut the door, then sped from the landing up five short steps and on into the bright sun-yellow kitchen where she thumped the bottle on a shelf in her pantry. The gleaming kitchen was U-shaped, with the open end separated from the dining room by a breakfast bar. The dining room opened onto the living room from which a hall extended the length of the upstairs portion of the house. Two bedrooms, a bath, and Loy's office at the back end were all more comfortable than showy. Downstairs, a sparsely furnished rec room—once Keith's prized domain—and the laundry area were next to the crowded garage.

Rays of bright May sunshine beckoned to Loy from the sliding glass doors that led from the dining room to the patio. She knew she should get back to balancing this month's assets and debits, but instead she poured herself another cup of coffee and wandered out to the patio to drink it.

Her house was a modest split-level in a typical suburban neighborhood on the Kansas side of the metropolis. The Saturday air reverberated with the sounds of children on bikes and roller skates, teenagers slamming car doors, mothers yelling, lawnmowers humming over yards. On any night in the summer tantalizing aromas of a barbecue floated through the street. It was a homey area, but what had really sold Keith and Loy on this house was the immense backyard, fenced with six-foot cedar pine, guaranteed to keep Jeeves out of trouble. She watched him now, lying on his side in the grass with his tongue hanging out. Bits of grass clung to his shaggy coat. Loy considered getting a brush and grooming him thoroughly. Instead, she lazily sipped her coffee.

The doorbell rang. Reluctantly Loy hoisted herself from the chaise and made her way through the tiled kitchen and down to the landing. As she opened the door she saw it was the delivery man who'd brought her the Dom Pérignon.

"Yes? Did you forget something?" she asked.

The young man grinned. "No, ma'am. Here you are." He handed her two more bottles and left, still grinning.

The tag on each one read . . . *and the next. . . .*

Two more bottles arrived each hour, disrupting Loy's work and ruffling her volatile temper. By two she nearly had a case of extremely expensive champagne. She definitely had a case of extremely frazzled nerves. After the first one all the tags had been the same. Hadn't Derett ever heard of overkill?

She wasn't able to keep her mind on her work. Each time the phone rang she leaped inches off the floor. Each time she told herself it was because she expected *New-Sports* to call, but each time she knew she was lying to herself. When she found herself doodling a series of D's in the corner of her accounting ledger, Loy clapped it forcefully shut. Stalking back to the kitchen, she tackled housecleaning. She vigorously scrubbed the bath and the kitchen first, then began dusting, attacking with the cloth as if charging a mortal foe.

At three she met the delivery man at the door before he had a chance to knock. He held out a single bottle.

"Is this it? Is this the last one?" she asked coldly.

The young man's smile wavered, then regathered force. "Yup." He started down her sidewalk, then paused. "Say, lady."

Loy looked up. "Yes?"

"He must be crazy about you," said the youth as he whisked away.

She slammed her front door shut and savagely tore the tag from its bright ribbon. Without reading it she marched to the kitchen, where she tossed it into the trash basket beneath the sink. A minute later she jerked open the cupboard and retrieved it.

Do you believe in love at first flight?

Her heart stopped for one full second. Then she forced it back to work as she angrily set the bottle with the others on her crammed pantry shelf. Derett had a lot to learn about her if he thought her the type to be bowled over by a few words scribbled on a card!

But that was precisely the problem. Loy was in danger of being bowled over by Derett Graham and she knew it. Had, in fact, known it from that first fleeting glimpse of his dazzling smile the evening before. Even, perhaps, before she'd even seen him. She remembered her goose bumps of fear and looked down at her arms to see them rising once more.

She eyed the bumps with resentment. It wasn't the champagne or the man's charm that filled her with dread. It wasn't even his mention of love, though that had been alarming enough. It was the aura of the man that she feared. Behind the engaging appeal, behind the sensual smiles and smoldering looks, Derett Graham clearly emitted the message, "I'm the serious kind." It scared Loy stiff.

Well, he wasn't going to get serious about her! She wouldn't give him the chance! There'd be no more flights with Mr. Graham, no, sir, uh-uh, she told herself in irritated resolution.

Loy's indignation carried her to the hall closet where she hauled out an ancient upright vacuum cleaner, a tight smile stretched over her lips. There was nothing, to her view, like vacuuming to release pent-up aggression. In this mood she didn't just run the machine across her worn celery-green carpet. She rammed it forcefully over the rug,

33

battering into baseboards and furniture with a mighty whack and thump. By the time she'd whacked and thumped her way into the dining room, her pique had faded.

Jeeves heard the noise and threw his paws against the patio doors, whoofing his demand to be allowed in to attack his detested enemy, the vacuum cleaner. The shrill ringing of the phone only increased the dog's ardent clamoring to be let in. Grabbing the wall phone by the refrigerator, Loy aimed her toes at the foot pedal of the vacuum and missed. Jeeves howled.

"Hello? What? Just a minute, please. *Shut up!* No, not you! My dog!" She shook her fist fiercely at the shaggy sheepdog, told him firmly to be quiet, finally hit the off pedal of her vacuum, and took a deep breath. "Yes?" she said pleasantly, while grimacing at the vague reflection of her poppy red tube-top and frayed cut-offs shimmering on the sliding glass door.

There was a long hesitation. "I think I may have the wrong number," said a male voice at last. "I was trying to call Cloud Sailing, Inc."

"This is Cloud Sailing, if you could hold the line a moment, please." She flung down the receiver, raced to her office, picked up the extension there, dashed back to hang up the kitchen phone, yelled at the still-barking Jeeves, and ran back down the hall. As she skidded to a halt at her desk she stubbed her toe, cursed, and puffed breathlessly into the mouthpiece, "May I help you?"

"Uh . . . Miss McDaniel?" the man asked uncertainly.

"Yes," huffed Loy, flipping open her appointment calendar.

"This is Jeff Reynolds of *NewSports* magazine."

Oh, no! She was definitely enrolling that dog in obedience school! Rubbing her bruised toe along the back of her calf, she assumed her most professional air. "Yes, Mr. Reynolds?"

"Keith Brenner recommended you," he began in tones

34

that clearly doubted Keith Brenner's recommendations. Within ten minutes, however, Loy's businesslike handling of the conversation reversed Reynolds's attitude. By the time they discussed lesson costs, he was even suggesting the magazine would rent the equipment they used at the Nationals in Iowa from Cloud Sailing.

"Umm, Mr. Reynolds," she said when he would have hung up. "Can you tell me why you'd go to the expense of training a journalist to do this? Why not just have a writer go up with a balloonist? Not," she quickly added, "that I don't want to train your writer. I do. I'm just . . . curious."

She wondered why he paused. It was almost imperceptible, but his hesitation was there. "Well," he explained after that brief delay, "we thought we'd get the real layman's point of view this way, make certain our readers experience the fresh excitement, the thrill of going from novice to actual pilot right along with our writer."

"Oh." Why did she feel dissatisfied? His explanation made sense. And why on earth was she questioning their reasons at all? The money was fabulous! "Well, I'll see your man on Monday then."

Loy hung up and danced gleefully around her crackerbox office, adroitly avoiding bumping into the black metal desk or matching file cabinet, the padded desk chair or wooden shelving that lined one wall. She tossed a mustard-colored cushion out of the round wicker chair and waltzed down to the kitchen and into the yard where she caught all seventy pounds of Jeeves into her arms with an "ooof." She whirled him back and forth happily while he cheerfully lapped at her chin. Money! She would have to have Keith and Jackie and their boy over for a dinner to celebrate. She'd have Lisle and Bill and their kids. She'd have Gary and the crew and, well, what the hell! She'd have a party!

After she calmed down she called Keith to report her good news. He whistled appreciatively and offered both his and Jackie's congratulations. She happily accepted their good wishes, then went to get ready for the evening's flight. Keith was, she decided, one lucky guy. Things had certainly worked out for him—he and Jackie were a great couple. Too bad things would never work out that way for her.

She shrugged off the wistful envy, determined to have nothing spoil her joyful day, and began planning what to wear for the meeting with her journalist. She and Reynolds had agreed that he would come by at about ten on Monday. It was only after she'd hung up that Loy realized she hadn't asked his name, but it didn't really matter. All that mattered was the income that would enable her to at long last pay off the Scout. The instruction fee plus the rental fees would perhaps even leave her some mad money to throw around.

As she flew over Royals Stadium that night, her passengers thrilled to be sailing over a near-capacity crowd at the baseball game, Loy daydreamed about meeting the *New-Sports* writer, about training him, about collecting her money, and most of all, about spending it. She was still debating between having the house painted or new carpeting laid in the living room when she dressed the following Monday morning.

Choosing the right clothing had been difficult. She'd thought at first of wearing a light beige linen suit with a peach blouse—the professional woman effect. But on second thought, she'd decided it didn't look active enough. She'd put on a denim jumpsuit styled like an aviator's flight suit, then promptly discarded it as being too aggressive. In the end she'd settled for being naturally sporty. She wore white pleated slacks with a bibbed sailor's top in hot pink crepe with quarter-length sleeves. She pulled her wheaten hair into an unruly pony tail which swung in a crinkling cascade to the middle of her back. Slipping her feet into leather clogs, she glanced at the clock radio beside her bed. It was ten exactly. She hoped he wouldn't be too late; she hated waiting for anyone or anything.

He wasn't. The chime of her doorbell announced his arrival just as she finished straightening the gathers of her blouse at the waist of her slacks. With the warmest welcoming smile on her lips, Loy threw open her front door. Her smile slithered down into a frown as she faced a camera lens she was coming to know only too well.

"What are you doing here?" she demanded with a snap that echoed the Nikon's shutter release.

"I've come to see you," replied Derett Graham, striding past her.

CHAPTER THREE

"You can't!" exclaimed Loy. She realized she was screeching to an empty foyer as Derett had already settled himself comfortably in her living room. She stormed up the steps after him. "Don't you dare sit down! I'm expecting someone—"

"We'll tell him—politely, of course—to get lost," returned Derett with an infuriating placidity. He lounged on her couch as if he intended to become a permanent fixture.

Loy ground her teeth. The worst of it was, despite her shock and annoyance, she'd felt a thrill shoot through her at the sight of him. The thrill had vanished almost immediately, but it had been there and that was enough to set her on edge. In a shrill voice quite unlike her own she demanded he leave.

The crinkles at the sides of his eyes deepened as he smiled with assurance. "If you get any angrier, you're going to be the color of your blouse. Which is, by the way, quite becoming." She sputtered with speechless fury as he cajoled her. "Come, sit down. I'll go after we've talked."

"Is there something wrong with your hearing, or is it your brain that's damaged?" inquired Loy pettishly. She moved into the room, but didn't sit. Glaring down at her unwanted guest, she said with even less warmth, "I am expecting someone. It's a business matter and I would appreciate it if you would leave before he arrives."

He nodded. "*NewSports* magazine."

She gaped at him, stunned. "How did you know that?"

38

Derett pulled a card from the pocket of his canary polo shirt. Wordlessly Loy reached to take it from his outstretched hand. Beneath the bold red logotype of the magazine was the name Derett Graham. "I free-lance quite a bit for them," he explained.

"You? *You're* the writer for *NewSports?*"

"Actually I have a confession to make," said Derett. He displayed the charming smile that emphasized the deep indentations beside his mouth. "This story is my idea."

"Your idea?" repeated Loy stupidly. The situation was spinning beyond her control and she had no idea how to stop it.

Derett shifted, propping an ankle on a knee and creasing what had been a well-pressed pair of tan slacks. He studied the array of plants arranged before the double window. His smile was still in place, but oddly enough, the dimples had disappeared. "Jeff Reynolds is my brother-in-law," he said slowly.

Her first impulse was to show him the door. Sanity, however, prevailed. She sank into the woven cane seat of her rocker and told herself the lure of the money couldn't be ignored. She refused to consider the possible lure of anything else. She wanted to tell him what a low-down opportunist she thought him. What she managed was an uneven, "Why?"

"For one thing, I happen to think it would make a great story for the magazine." He paused and suddenly the dimples reappeared in a radiant show of appeal. "For another, I very much want to get to know you. I want to know you very well."

Loy knew how a rabbit must feel when it couldn't find a hole to bolt down. She glanced around her living room, not seeing any of the too-familiar furnishings, only too aware of the man her gaze so diligently avoided. She knew without looking that those deep green eyes were fastened on her, questing, probing. The intensity of his gaze could be felt across the width of her worn carpet. Like a spider poised at the center of his web, he was waiting to strike. Her muscles tensed even as her nerves capered. She had to stay free of that intricate tangle; she had to.

"Why?" she asked again, this time sounding like a creaky hinge.

"That's a strange question for a lovely—a very lovely—lady to ask. If you have to put labels on it, I guess you'd say it was attraction. All I know is from the moment I saw you, I felt I had to get to know you."

She leaped to her feet, clenching her hands together to keep them from trembling visibly. "Let's get something straight. This is a business arrangement, nothing else. I train you for your BPC, then you go write your story. If you want something more than that, get yourself another pilot. I'm not available for outside activities—of any kind."

She attempted to stare him down, but her gaze wavered, then fell as he came lithely to his feet. Her capitulation instantly angered her. She recovered and lifted her eyes to glower at him. Even with the additional height of her clogs, she had to tilt her head to fix her frown on him; the slight disadvantage simply irritated her further. But it was the complacency she saw stamped over his handsome features that really fueled her increasing anger.

"What's a BPC?" he inquired in a mild tone that made Loy long to kick his shin.

"A Balloon Pilot Certificate. The pilot's license required by the FAA." She spoke in short, sharp bursts.

Her anger apparently didn't bother him. He wandered past her into the dining room, running his hand over the scarred wood of the old oak table she'd found at an estate sale and refinished herself. He didn't look at her; his eyes roamed the room, glancing into the kitchen as he meandered about. "How long will it take to get that?"

"It depends on various factors," she replied. Her ire was dissipating. How could she stay angry when he wouldn't cooperate and fight back? And why did she feel let down?

After all, he was keeping the conversation on business. That should please her. "You need ten instructed flying hours—and when you get them in depends on the weather. There's also a checkout flight and an hour solo flight required, as well as written and oral exams."

"When can we start?"

"I—well—I'll loan you a couple of books to read. Then you should come with us on charters and put in several hours learning about crewing and chasing. Actually, being a student is rather like an apprenticeship. You learn mostly by doing."

He was at the patio doors now, looking out over her yard. She followed him, but didn't realize until he had it open that he was sliding back the glass door.

"Don't! My dog—" she sputtered uselessly as he stepped out onto the concrete patio.

He turned and smiled at her. "Nice yard," he said, then frowned at her expression of horror. An enormous whoof echoed behind him. He whirled at the sound. From out of the shadow of a large maple a flying mass of gray and white fur hurtled toward them, growling and barking. Loy covered her face with her hands as Jeeves sprang forward.

"Sit!" commanded Derett.

Instead of the yap and thud she expected to hear, Loy heard a shrill whine. She peeked through her fingers, then slowly lowered her hands in astonishment. Jeeves sat before Derett, eyes pleading as he whimpered hopefully. Derett held his hand out, palm down, then swiftly reversed it to chuck the dog under the chin. "Good boy, good boy," he said with approval. "This is a good dog you have."

Loy knew her mouth was hanging open, but she couldn't shut it. Jeeves obeyed no one, no one at all, ever. Not even Keith or Gary, both of whom dwarfed Derett in size. Her amazement turned to annoyance. She gave her dog the look of contemptuous scorn and hurt one gave a beloved traitor, then addressed Derett coolly. "Isn't he though? Now, if you'll excuse me, I'll get those books for you."

She whisked away before he could say anything, muttering all the way to her office. She decided she should have named the beast Judas, not Jeeves. How had he done it? She said sit to that dog and he thought it meant jump! Loy continued to steam as she pawed over her bookshelves. By the time she located the two manuals and one colorful history of ballooning, she was a mass of righteous indignation.

Back out on the patio she found her dog happily fetching a rubber toy for Derett. She slapped the books onto the top of a black gas grill. "Here you are," she said with bare civility.

Derett turned. Tilting his head, he deliberately looked her over from head to toe, raising his brows at each of her curves. Her skin began to tingle, her pulse to pound. She'd have thought it impossible to shudder from the force of a mere look. She found it was very possible indeed. His darkening gaze might as well have been an intimate caress. Loy felt her nipples extend as he brought his eyes back to the swell of her breasts; she could only hope the square sailor bib hid that from his view.

"You're the color of your blouse again," he commented. "I can't say that hot pink suits your skin as well as it does the top."

Because he spoke with such friendly warmth, Loy once again lost her protective anger. While at the back of her mind she told herself she was walking into danger, she was unable to resist returning his smile.

"That's better," he said in much the same tones he'd praised Jeeves. He came forward and lifted the first book off the stack. "*The Ballooning Digest,*" he read aloud, flipping it open.

While he scanned the pages Loy watched him, noticing how broad his shoulders were in relation to the slimness of his waist and hips. It was precisely the type of thing she least wanted to notice about him, the type of thing to send shivers of fear racing down her spine. Needing to escape the disturbing proximity of him, she sidled to the doors. "How about something to drink?"

He glanced from the book in his hand to her and she was startled at how brilliant his eyes could be. He grinned. "What do you have that sparkles?"

She studied the humor curving his mouth and wished she could recall the anger she'd felt when receiving the champagne. Instead she smiled ruefully. "Don't you think you were a bit excessive?"

He shrugged. "Do you?"

"Yes," she replied with an emphatic nod. "What are you—rich as Croesus?"

"Hardly," he chuckled, and she couldn't help liking the warm melody of the sound. "But I think of all the joy of sharing each bottle with you and I consider it money well spent."

"You think wrong," she said with a defiant thrust of her chin. "We won't be sharing anything beyond a few lessons."

"Don't you believe in it then?"

Her brows drew together in wary puzzlement. "Believe in what?"

"Love at first flight," he answered with a crooked smile.

She turned away quickly, the long stream of her hair crackling as it whisked through the air. The low suggestion in his voice, the sensual appeal in his smile, the hungry desire in his eyes, burst through her veins like liquid flames. "No. I don't believe in love of any kind," she stated flatly as she retreated into the kitchen.

Sunlight checkered the tile floor and trapped the shadow of the man behind her. Loy glanced over her shoulder, dismayed to see Derett had followed her. She yanked open a cupboard to get glasses and slammed it shut as Jeeves scratched at the door, emitting a howling protest at being

43

left out of the party. "Damn that dog!" muttered Loy in a release of nervous emotion.

To her surprise Derett strode to the patio doors, where the dog continued to yowl mournfully. He rapped the glass once loudly, and said firmly, "Stop. Sit, Jeeves." Again he motioned downward with his hand, palm flat. Again Jeeves sat, eyeing them sadly but quietly through the glass.

"Are you a magician?" asked Loy with a tinge of resentment as he returned to the gleaming cheeriness of the kitchen.

"No, just unwilling to tolerate his disobedience. Dogs, like children, can sense when you don't intend to put up with their misbehavior."

"Too bad you're not a dog," she said with a flash of humor. "Maybe you could sense what I won't put up with."

His dimples quirked. "Oh, I don't know . . . maybe I could. But I'm certain I'd be smart enough to ignore it."

She occupied herself with pouring iced tea into two tall glasses, glad to be able to keep her back to him. The sight of him was continuing to have an unwarranted and unwanted effect upon her. The mere tilt of his lips had accelerated her pulse to a ridiculous degree. As she dropped ice cubes into a glass and handed it to him, she inquired in what she hoped were noncommittal tones, "Why did you have your brother-in-law contact Keith Brenner? Why not call me direct?"

Their fingers grazed as he took the glass. Loy jerked back and instantly wished she hadn't. She didn't want him to so much as suspect how flustered he was making her feel. She clenched her glass tightly, as if it might safely anchor her in the whirling vortex of her confused emotions.

"I didn't tell Jeff to contact anyone specifically," he replied easily. "I just asked him to make the offer as legit

44

as possible. I had the feeling that if you suspected that I was involved, you'd pass it up, no matter how lucrative."

He was right, she would have. But Loy had no intention of giving him the satisfaction of knowing that. He was looking too darned satisfied as it was. "Umm," she murmured as she sipped her tea. She nearly spewed it out when he shot her a sharp look and went on. "I didn't even know Brenner—or that he was your ex—until Jeff told me about the call."

"Oh," was her glorious comeback when she ceased choking on her tea.

"Were you married long?"

"Awhile," she answered shortly. "Now, when would you like to begin your lessons, Mr. Graham?"

"Derett. And as soon as possible. Now, if you like." He smiled, seeming to accept her refusal to discuss her marriage. But that, thought Loy with a chill prickling, was just the problem. He *seemed* to accept it. She knew with dread certainty that he didn't. The knowledge made her quiver.

"That isn't necessary, or even possible," she said. A thin stretch of her mouth passed for a smile. "I suggest you read over those books and then accompany me on a charter."

"Do you have a charter tonight?" She nodded reluctantly and he flashed his dimples at her. "Great. I'll come along."

She looked away from the radiance of that smile. "All right. Call me between four and five and I'll tell you where to meet us if the weather's cooperating."

He agreed and thanked her for the tea as he collected the books. She walked with him to the door, but paused before opening it. She had to set things straight, now, before it got out of hand. "Mr. Graham?"

"Derett."

"Don't expect anything more than instruction from me. I'm not willing to give it."

45

She threw open the door and sped away before he could respond. The door clicked shut as she withdrew into the safety of her office, the sanctum when all others failed. She heard the start of an engine, listened as it faded into the distance. At least she'd given him fair warning! The thought only depressed her the more. She knew he'd ignore the truth of her warning. Working with him would be about as sensible as playing with matches in a petroleum plant.

More than ever she believed that Derett Graham spelled trouble, big trouble. He was rushing her, and being rushed frightened Loy. She'd been involved with men who rushed her before, with disastrous results. She didn't understand what attracted Derett so powerfully to her. Didn't he see the freckles? Couldn't he see her brow was too wide, her cheekbones too high, her face too angular? She wasn't plain, she admitted that, but she certainly wasn't a *femme fatale*. There were men who seemed to recognize this. Since her second divorce she'd led an active enough social life, dating, even enjoying deeper relationships when they didn't involve fettering entanglements. But here was Derett, like Stan and Keith before him, wanting to grab hold of her on sight.

But this time there was a difference. This time Loy was no longer naïve or vulnerable. This time Loy wouldn't fall into the trap waiting to spring heartbreak on her. She would resist the charm of Derett Graham and keep her heart whole.

On that determined thought Loy began to immerse herself in her work, but was almost immediately distracted by the ringing of the doorbell. She stamped forcefully toward it, certain it would be Derett returning to plague her yet again. She flung open the door and choked back her intended disagreeable greeting.

"My, don't you look fierce!" exclaimed her sister as she entered. With the ease of one who expects to be welcomed,

Lisle strolled up into the kitchen, the skirt of her periwinkle sundress flaring with her softly swaying movement.

When they were younger, people had often mistaken the McDaniel sisters for twins. They were of much the same height and build, with long, classical necks and exquisitely fine bone structures, but Loy had never had the natural seductiveness of her elder sister, and as they grew older, the error was made less frequently. Lisle's hair was not the muted gold of a wheatfield, but the red-amber of melted honey, and, unlike Loy's, her eyes weren't like the sea, changing color with each mood. They were a clear, cool, spring-water blue, never clouded with unhappiness. Lisle McDaniel Craeger breathed the confident contentment that her younger sister exhibited, but did not truly feel.

Trailing behind Lisle into the kitchen, Loy's scowl faded into a smile. "So what's up?" she asked.

"For me? Nothing. The kids went off to school this morning and after inhaling the wondrous sound of silence I got lonely. I thought you could fix me lunch." Lisle perched on one of the stools at the breakfast bar, leaning her tanned arms on the counter. Her hair draped gracefully to her bare shoulders, her long legs crossed at the ankles. She looked, as always, competently cool. Loy expected that her sister would look just the same traversing Death Valley on foot.

"Such a deal," Loy laughed as she opened her refrigerator. "How could I possibly refuse? Not that I have much to offer. Does a bologna sandwich sound appetizing?"

"Anything I don't have to fix—and anything that doesn't have peanut butter in it—is great with me. What is it about kids' stomachs that allows them to digest tons of that stuff?" Lisle wrinkled her nose at the thought, all the while watching Loy putter about, collecting knives, mayonnaise, bread. She tipped her head, and her blue eyes narrowed. "You look terrific. Is that top new?"

47

"Yes. It was a lucky find, on sale at Halls." She pulled out a head of lettuce and held it up. Lisle nodded.

"Any reason you're so dressed up?"

"I had a business appointment this morning," replied Loy evasively. She didn't want to expand on it. She didn't want her sister to get any ridiculous ideas. Lisle was endlessly matchmaking for her. Until proven unworthy, Lisle considered every male a matrimonial prospect for her baby sister; she was forever thrusting men in Loy's direction. And nothing Loy could say or do seemed to deter Lisle from her ultimate goal of sending her baby sister marching down the aisle one more time.

Heaping potato chips on bright blue plastic plates, Loy changed the subject by asking about Bill's recent promotion. With a sharp look that conveyed her understanding of the diversionary tactic, Lisle obediently launched into glowing praise of her husband. She then detailed the latest escapades of her two children, Becky and Jason, aged eight and five respectively. They moved from that to Loy's plans for a barbecue party once school was out. But after they'd eaten and cleared away the last of the dishes, Lisle returned like a homing pigeon, just as Loy had feared she would, to the one topic she most wished to avoid.

"So this appointment you had," Lisle drawled provocatively, "tell me about him."

"How do you know it was with a male? There are two sexes, you know."

"I know by the scowl you were wearing when I arrived. There isn't a woman in the world who could make you frown like that—"

"Except you," cut in Loy.

"Except me," agreed Lisle with a ready laugh. "But it usually takes a man to really rile you. So tell me about him. Was he good looking?"

"Will you please stop inspecting every man on the street for possibilities as my next mate? How many times do I have to tell you that I don't need or want one? I'm perfectly happy with my life as it is!"

"Are you?"

The short query struck Loy painfully. She sucked in her breath and studied the swirls in the Formica countertop. "Don't you think it's possible to get through life without a man?" she inquired somewhat shrilly.

"For some women, yes. For you, no." Lisle reached out and set her fingers lightly on Loy's arm. "You're not made that way any more than I am, and you never will be. It's been nearly three years since you and Keith split up. It's past time you thought about settling down again."

Loy laughed, a bitter crack that echoed erratically like a gunshot. "How can you equate marriage with settling down? Especially in my case?"

"When you find the right man—"

"I don't want to find any man!" interrupted Loy heatedly. "Don't you ever listen to me? I just said I'm perfectly content as I am. Single."

"It's not natural. Just because you've been thrown once or twice—"

"This isn't like getting back up on a horse, Lisle! I did that once and look what happened. I took five years from a very nice guy—"

"You gave a lot to Keith and you know it."

"But he'd have been happier with someone else. Look how happy he is with Jackie. Okay, okay," said Loy, slapping her hands on her knees at the look in her sister's eyes, "so maybe he wouldn't have been so happy with her if he hadn't had the years with me. But the five years were a mistake, Lisle. One I do not intend to ever repeat."

They'd had that argument so many times they each knew the responses by heart, or so it seemed to Loy. She was weary of it. It was obvious that she wasn't suited for marriage; she couldn't understand why anyone who claimed to care about her would be so anxious to see her make another monumental mess of her life.

As if sensing she'd pushed her sister to the limit, Lisle now stood and crossed the room to the pantry. "I'll make us some old-fashioned lemonade, if you still have the—" She broke off as she stared at the bottles of champagne standing in two neat rows along the middle shelf. She picked one up. "Dom Pérignon! How on earth could you afford this, sis?"

Loy scurried to the cupboard beside the sink. Keeping her back to her sister's probing eyes, she pulled glasses down to the counter and admitted reluctantly, "I couldn't. They were a gift."

"A gift? Someone gave you an entire case of Dom Pérignon?" Speculation gleamed in Lisle's eyes. "Who?"

"Oh, a charter I took up a couple of nights ago." Her attempt to sound lightly casual went over like a lead balloon. Lisle pounced instantly.

"Who? Have you seen him since? Are you dating?"

Gritting her teeth, Loy gave in to the inevitable and told her sister about Derett Graham and the assignment for *NewSports* magazine. When Lisle demanded to know what Derett was like, Loy shrugged. "Tall and tanned. A gorgeous hunk of a man. His smile would melt iron bars at twenty paces."

"But not you, is that it?"

"That's it," she averred, telling herself it was the truth. "And don't think otherwise, sister, dear. You'll only be disappointed if you do."

"It's not my disappointment that matters. I wish I could convince you of that." Lisle sighed and looped her hair back behind her ears. "I have to be going. I promised Mom and Dad I'd drive out to Lakewood to see them today."

"Next time let's go over the arrangements for my barbecue rather than my very dull, nonexistent love life," suggested Loy with some return to humor as she walked her sister to her car. She instructed Lisle to give the folks her love, then waved good-bye, feeling a guilty relief to see her go.

Lisle's obvious excitement over the champagne disturbed Loy. It reminded her of the danger of being involved with the man. Even if she accepted the attraction she felt for Derett, it would only mean another chance at heartbreak. After all, she wasn't exactly an authority on how to keep a man happy. It was painfully obvious that she didn't wear well on acquaintance. Hadn't that been proved often enough?

CHAPTER FOUR

Westering sunlight glazed the rutted pavement, highlighting jagged crevices and buckling cracks. Tall grass hedged the narrow country road, bending in the breeze. Across a wide swatch Loy and Gary looked at each other and simultaneously shook their heads.

They tramped through the field back to the Scout. "Too many sticklers here," Loy explained with a reassuring smile to the young couple waiting in the back seat. She didn't look beyond them, didn't look to the trio riding in the trailer. She'd managed to avoid the trailer since Derett Graham had joined the Perren brothers there at the outset of the evening. "We'll drive on a bit. I think I know where we'll find a perfect launch site."

They jolted onward, turning onto a major road out beyond the limits of the city, stretching toward DeSoto, Kansas. Loy drove without speaking, her eyes busily searching the rural roadside while her mind busily reviewed her earlier exchange with Derett. She'd scarcely been able to think of anything else since he climbed into the trailer.

He'd met them as arranged, at a local quick-stop shop. He was leaning casually against the side of the brick building sipping a soda. As they pulled to a halt he straightened and aimed a perfect loop shot of the can into a large trash barrel, then sauntered toward them. Tight, faded jeans stretched tautly against his long legs as he moved; the canary knit shirt seemed to strain against his solid physique. The ubiquitous Nikon hung over his shoulder and, seeing it, Loy wondered if he made love with the damn thing slung around his neck. She caught herself up on the thought, somewhat disconcerted to have even briefly considered such a thing. Angry with herself, she greeted him brusquely.

"We'll be meeting our charter here," she said without preamble as she climbed out of the Scout. "Then we'll drive out toward DeSoto for our flight. You can get in back with Roger and Danny."

He didn't move toward the trailer. Instead, when she began walking toward the store, he fell into step beside her. For three strides she paid no attention. On the fourth she stopped abruptly and focused an inquiring glare at him. He smiled confidently. She had the feeling he knew he was getting to her, he knew it and liked it.

"You need something?" she asked in tones that clearly didn't invite an answer.

"Well, now that you mention it . . ." he drawled as he eyed the length of her figure, pausing at each curve along the way.

Loy gnashed her teeth. "What does it take to get a message through to you? I told you, all you're getting from me is flight instruction. Period. No added fringes of any kind."

"So instruct me."

"This isn't a joke!"

"I'm not joking." He spread his hands in a placating gesture. "Instead of blowing up at me, you might tell me where you're going."

Once again he'd knocked the wind from her sails. She knew she'd overreacted, letting her personal fears cloud her usual good sense. He seemed to have a knack for unhinging her without doing anything at all. She looked away from the tilt of his half-smile, feeling more than a little absurd. When he was this close, she felt curiously unable to resist his allure. With effort Loy gathered her scattered wits and explained, "I'm going to use the phone. To call the flight service."

"What's that?"

"It's a weather service. You call before your flight, give your identifying number and where you intend to fly, and they give you the weather conditions, wind speed, and direction at the nearest airport."

"You call before every flight?"

Both the question and his tone were reasonable. So why did she feel this unreasonable edginess? Not daring to look at him, she nodded. "Always. No matter how good the weather appears to be, there's always a chance a front is moving in."

They walked together to the pay phone near the door of the small store. Loy had always considered herself to be all legs. During the unbearable gangliness of adolescence, she'd often wished she could hack off two or three inches from thigh to calf. Now she noted how Derett's strides matched her own for length, how his own legs seemed to outstretch hers. Not, of course, she hastily told herself, that that meant anything at all.

She dug into the pocket of her olive hiking shorts and pulled out a dime, then reached for the phone. Derett's hand came down over hers, pressing her palm into the cool plastic of the receiver, covering her fingers with the warmth of his skin.

"What are you afraid of?" he asked quietly.

Her heart trip-hammered into action. She stared at the browned fingers curling over her flesh and stuttered, "A-afraid? Don't be ridiculous!"

"If you're not afraid, why do you look at me as if I'm about to suck your blood? I'm not Dracula, just a guy who wants to know you." His voice had dropped to a rustle.

If he had shouted, his words couldn't have rung more clearly in her ears. She gave him precisely the horrified stare he'd described and he slowly released her hand. "There, you see," he said, sounding reproachful. "That's what I'm talking about. Is it men in general or just me that you fear so much?"

Loy just barely restrained herself from running. Calling upon every reserve of strength she possessed, she managed a steady response. "Your ego, Mr. Graham, is only exceeded by your vivid imagination. I don't fear men and I certainly don't fear you."

Though she'd changed for the flight into shorts and a cream cotton top, she'd left her hair in the ponytail of the morning; Derett now caught the long rippling wave of it. Splaying his fingers, he let the ends trickle from his grasp. "I will know you, Loy. Whether you think you fear me or not."

Before she could contradict this arrogant assumption, he spun away to join Danny and Roger slouching by the trailer. When she was able to make her fingers function, she punched the proper phone buttons to make her call to the service. By the time she received the go-ahead on the weather, the young couple who had chartered the flight had arrived and they immediately set off to find a launch site.

Since then, Loy could think of little beyond the harsh memory of Derett's low voice telling her in no uncertain terms that he would know her. Her stomach fluttered continually, rather like it had on the night of her very first flight.

On the horizon full-leaved trees rimmed a vast stretch of cloudless blue. Loy turned left before reaching the trees, pulling into a graveled lot beside a square, one-story brick building. She drove onward, easing over cement bumps to finally park in an empty, flat, mowed field. She got out, then held back the seat for her passengers to exit.

While her husband grinned broadly in anticipation, the young woman played nervously with the frizzy ends of her dark hair. Loy had learned long ago that the best way to handle the nervous types was to give them something to do. She signaled for the pair to follow her as she moved

55

back to the trailer. Gary was there ahead of them, already filling a small balloon with helium from a tank at the back. As they came forward, Loy heard Derett remark on the property rights of the schoolyard.

"We call it balloonists' privilege," responded Gary easily. "When necessary, ignore all signs and boundaries."

"So balloonists make their own rules. I'll have to remember that," drawled Derett as he fixed a meaningful look on Loy.

She cast him a withering glare in return, but he merely met it with a smile. It was the lopsided smile, the one which softened the structure of his face with two deep dimples. She whirled away from the force of it, wrenching the small orange balloon from Gary's hand and thrusting it toward her nervous passenger. "Please, hold this, Carrie, until we tell you to let it go."

With a nod of her dark head Carrie gripped the balloon as though grasping hold of a lifeline. Gary ambled toward the front of the vehicle to fumble through the glove compartment and Loy began speaking in a cool voice to Derett. "We set off the balloon, then follow its progress with a sighting compass. That way we can see the directions the balloon travels, the strength of the wind, changes in current, and so forth. As you may know, winds blow in different directions at different altitudes."

Gary returned with an instrument that looked like an Instamatic camera; Carrie was told to let the helium balloon go while he watched it fly away through the compass. Directly after that the hectic business of getting aloft began. Loy had just bolted her instrument panel into place when she noticed Derett pulling on the nylon as he helped Roger spread the envelope over the grass. She immediately came up beside him. "We spread by holding on to a certain cable, pulling on *it* rather than the fabric. If you pull on the fabric, the nylon could rip."

Holding on to the steel line, she stepped backward, stretching the fabric flat. Derett nodded, then slanted the

56

length of his body against her back and clasped his hand over hers. "Like this?" he asked with angelic innocence.

The solid tension of his musculature compressed against her, stunning her into immobility. For a fraction of a heartbeat, she felt the softness of her buttocks backed into the hardness of his groin. Then her senses returned fully, and she snatched her hands free and skittered away from him. "Yes," she snapped.

Stalking away, she heard his low chuckle. She scowled so fiercely as she came up to the gondola that her passengers took two steps back. She saw their reaction and for the second time that night Loy pulled herself up short. It was going to be a long, long time between the first of May and the last of July if she didn't get a hold of herself. Fixing a smile on her face, she went back to work, determined to quit reacting like a candidate for a padded cell.

When all the steel lines had been attached to the basket and the blower fan brought forward, Gary held the crown line and Roger weighted the basket. Loy knelt before the tipped-over gondola and tersely told Dan and Derett to hold the envelope mouth open. She paused and stared a challenge at Derett.

"Don't let go of the envelope until I say so. It will get hot and you may think I'm going to burn you, but I won't."

He raised his brows, the scarred one tilting unevenly. "I'm not the one who's afraid."

He'd picked up the gauntlet she'd thrown and tossed it back at her. Loy looked away, biting back her urge to retort sharply. She had a job to do. She hit the blast valve, sending a stream of flame into the rising balloon. Inside, the balloon was a kaleidoscopic tent wavering to hoist itself. Loy focused on it, on the struggle to get into the air, in an effort to ignore the man anchoring the skirt. In a few minutes the balloon rocked free of the men's grip, the basket was heaved upright, and the two passengers were hustled in.

As they slowly lifted into the wind, Loy's attention was given to the burner, hitting the valve in short bursts. The heat clung to her skin. It was, however, nothing compared to the inner heat spreading through her veins. She glanced down and saw the foursome on the ground, saw the sandy hair and yellow shirt of one, then returned her gaze upward.

"Wow, this is great, awesome," whistled Jerry. His wife nodded a tense, uncertain agreement and Loy murmured, "Yes, isn't it?" without really knowing what she'd said. This was one flight that was overshadowed by the chase taking place below. As they passed fields plowed like narrow-wale corduroy and treetops matted like thick rugs, Loy followed the progress of the Scout on the paved strands winding through the countryside with deeper than usual interest. Though not generally given to self-deception, she refused to consider the reasons for this uncommon absorption in her crew.

She was trying so hard to avoid thoughts of him, it was a shock to abruptly hear Derett's voice crackle over the CB radio. "Cloud Chaser here. Come in, cap'n, wherever you are."

For one second she eyed the radio as if it had bitten her. Then she inhaled deeply and responded in what she hoped were normal tones. "Sixteen to Cloud Chaser. What do you need?"

"What's up ahead?" asked Derett.

She paused, hearing the smile in his voice. Did he smile at everything, she wondered peevishly. The answer came before the question departed. Yes. He was the type to enjoy what he was doing or he wouldn't do it. His enjoyment of life, of himself, both enticed Loy and evoked her envy. She firmly quashed any further musings about him and looked out over the landscape. She could see the vehicle poised at the cross of a T in the road. "You're facing a dead end," she said tersely. "Turn left and go straight until the next cross-section, then turn right."

"Got it," he said, and the radio went silent.

By the end of the ninety-minute flight, Carrie had calmed, Jerry had fallen in love with the sport, and Loy had convinced herself that whatever fascination Derett Graham exerted over her was nothing she couldn't handle. He was, after all, nothing more than an attractive man. In the past three years she'd known men just as attractive and escaped unharmed, hadn't she?

The landing was nearly perfect, a light touchdown with only minor rocking on a clear field easily accessible to the highway. Pink dashed the sky and dappled the verdant grass around them with warnings of the impending sunset. A merry staccato horn announced the arrival of the chasers and Loy greeted her crew with a wide, smug grin that sent her freckles dancing over her face.

"Not bad, boss," chuckled Gary.

"Not bad, huh! It was great!" she returned.

"Great flight, great pilot," drawled Derett.

"Even for a lady?" Her voice was laden with sarcasm.

"*Especially* for a lady." He suddenly snapped to attention and brought his hand to his brow. "I salute you, cap'n."

Certain he was mocking her, Loy spun around and began issuing instructions to Dan and Roger. She heard Derett walk away, but didn't look to see where he went. She fully intended to ignore him for the rest of the night.

She discovered Derett Graham was not a man one could ignore. Long before she let off the excess propane, Derett began making his presence known. The continual clicking of his camera told her precisely where he was and, worse, that he was following her progress every step of the way. The balloon was deflated, permeating the air with the odor of heated fabric. Bugs skittered past as air was rolled out of the envelope, lines were taped and unhooked, uprights and instruments removed. And still the echoing snap of a shutter shadowed Loy. The sound drummed in her blood until finally she swung to face him.

"Will you stop that?" she angrily demanded.

Lowering his camera, he tilted his head to study her. "Why does this bother you so much?"

"I don't know. It just does," she muttered, already regretting her outburst.

"Maybe it's not the camera that's bothering you at all," he said softly. He slid forward, a whisper away, and suggested huskily, "Maybe it's the photographer."

"Don't be ridiculous!" she denied too quickly.

"That's twice tonight you've said that. But, you know, somehow I don't think I'm the one being ridiculous . . ."

The heat of his breath nuzzled her neck. Loy jerked back, needing to be away from him, away from his disconcerting magnetism. She took a step, but halted as he called out to her. With reluctance she looked over her shoulder at him. He appeared, for once, solemnly serious.

"You're being paid—and very well, I might add—to put up with me and my camera. Whatever you think you have to fear, you accepted the situation when you accepted Jeff's offer. If you'll stop cringing from the lens, I promise I won't use any photos without your consent. Fair enough?"

She opened her mouth, then closed it. What could she say? She couldn't object. He was right. She was being paid very well indeed to put up with him. And his camera. With a short nod of agreement, she strode off.

As soon as the balloon was packed into its sleeve and the basket covered in the trailer, Loy uncorked the chilled champagne and approached the couple who couldn't stop talking about their experience.

"Now for the celebration," she said. "If you'll stand together here, I wish to say a few words." She recited a poem about the wind, the sun, and the earth, sprinkling bits of grass atop their heads, then baptizing them with a trickle of champagne. Handing them the bottle with congratulations, she slipped away to mark the flight in her log.

60

She sat on the passenger side, her feet propped against the open car door and her log flat on her lap. A shadow fell across the page and she paused, knowing without looking who stood there.

"That was an interesting ceremony," he remarked.

She didn't take the bait he dangled. Calmly finishing her logging, she agreed simply. "Yes, it is."

"Perhaps not as . . . saturating . . . as mine."

Loy closed her book and capped her pen. She set both on the dashboard. Finally she raised her eyes. "I guess I owe you an apology."

To her surprise Derett grinned. "It's not necessary. So far as I'm concerned, bathing in champagne's not a bad way to start a relationship."

Didn't he ever lose his temper? She stood up. "How odd. I wouldn't have said that we had a relationship."

"Wrong again," he murmured as she strode past him.

The stiffening of her spine was imperceptible. Only she knew how much he disturbed her. Only she knew how much she was beginning to secretly enjoy it.

It had been years since Loy had felt the sheer electric thrill of being pursued by a man who physically excited her. Simply being around Derett roused her. Tonight the air had seemed more alive, the sky brighter and bluer, the sounds and smells sharper. Her fingertips had been attuned to the textures and shapes of objects like never before. It was both stimulating and shocking. She didn't want to feel more alive around Derett. She didn't want to feel anything around him, period.

With as much a show of normalcy as she could muster, Loy gathered her crew and passengers together for the drive back into town. Still reliving each detail of their flight, Jerry and Carrie seated themselves in the back. Loy settled behind the wheel, listening to them in amusement. Her amusement vanished as she realized it wasn't Gary who'd just climbed in beside her.

Derett leaned into the corner of the seat, bracing his

shoulder against the door as he steadily watched Loy maneuver onto the highway. It took all her will not to yell at him to stop staring. She focused on the road ahead, but could not ignore the stretch of leg invading her periphery. That length of faded denim tightly hugging muscle and bone was very symbolic. He was invading her life, sliding in and taking over, just as he was inching into her side vision. Loy determined she would not deign to notice him and instantly, perversely, glanced in his direction. He curved his lips in a knowing smile and her eyes snapped back to the road.

"What did you think of your first time at crewing?" she asked, then wondered why she'd said anything at all. She hadn't meant to.

"Is it always such organized confusion?" he asked in reply.

She had to grin at that. "Always," she confirmed. Still smiling, she asked, "Anything in particular you wondered about?"

"Well, there was one major surprise." He paused provocatively and Loy could feel his eyes on her.

"Yes?" she prodded curtly. "What was it?"

"You didn't burn me."

She eyed him suspiciously. He met her look directly. She quickly slid her gaze away. "Of course not."

"Well, I wasn't sure . . ." He shifted, bending his knee at an angle over the seat and resting his hand on his kneecap. "You looked as if you longed to do it. The fabric got damned hot—my fingers were stinging—and I thought, *She tips that burner even slightly and I'm done for. Roast Derett à la McDaniel.*"

He spoke lightly, teasingly. Loy said nothing. It was becoming increasingly difficult for her not to respond to his warmth. He infuriated her one moment and intrigued her the next. But Loy knew she couldn't risk involvement with him. The mere thought of his eventual disillusionment with her, of the inevitable failure of their relationship, was unbearable. The actuality of it would crush her. She'd been through that particular kind of hell twice. A third time would destroy her. With a heavy sigh she again resolved to remain impersonal toward him.

The low murmur of voices from the back seat drifted forward to emphasize the length of their own silence. All the while, Loy was vividly conscious of the man beside her. If she'd been asked whether the sunset was pink or purple or a bright burst of orange, she'd have stared blankly and said she couldn't say. But if asked what shades of blue melted together in the denim of Derett's jeans, she'd have promptly answered, "Powder at the knee, radiating to a deep perse down the leg." She could have ticked off the navy of his socks, the grass stains on his gray canvas shoes, even the varying shades of tan along his arm and the fine gold of the hair dusting it. The fact that she could have recited all this filled her with dismay. She stared straight ahead and knew she was a fool.

After a time Derett remarked casually, "Overall I really enjoyed myself tonight. Even when I didn't understand what was going on, my adrenaline was pumping with excitement. When that magnificent-colored globe lifted into the sky, I felt . . . fulfilled."

It was an expression of Loy's own feelings. As stirring as piloting was, she'd always felt an unbeatable charge of achievement when crewing. Without realizing it she gave him one of her friendliest smiles. "I know just what you mean," she agreed readily.

The tension slowly eased as they passed the remainder of the ride in a discussion of procedures and principles involved in getting a hot air balloon aloft. When they'd parked at the convenience store, the neon lights speckling them in crimson shadows, Loy accepted the effusion of thanks from her passengers with a sincere smile. Gary and the Perrens also said good night and departed amid a series of waves. Alone again, Loy turned to Derett, feeling something akin to cordiality toward him.

"We're scheduled for a charter every night for the rest of the week," she explained. "If you call around four or five each day, I can let you know if we're going, then if you want to crew that night, we'll arrange where to meet."

"Was your divorce messy?" he inquired in return.

The unexpected question threw her totally off-balance. She was grateful she was holding on to the open door of the Scout, because she'd have fallen over otherwise. She could only stare at him in open-mouthed surprise.

"Did Brenner leave you with a bad taste for men?" he pressed.

That spurred her into speech. "Keith?" she squeaked in disbelief. "Keith?"

Derett frowned. In the darkening light his sandy hair held the glow of the flickering neon. She could just see the lines etched in his brow as he peered into her features. "What did he do to you? Why are you—"

"Not that it's any of your business," cut in Loy stiffly. She had no intention of discussing her personal life with this man. "But I assure you Keith Brenner is a kind, wonderfully loving man. My marriage with him didn't leave me with a bad taste for his type of man at all."

"If he's so wonderful, why did—"

"That's the last time I intend to discuss Keith with you. It's really none of your business. Now, if you want to crew tomorrow night, call me at five."

She pivoted to scramble into the driver's seat, but Derett shot out a hand to hold her back. "It is my business, Loy. I intend to make anything to do with you my business."

"Where do you get off—" she flared, only to be silenced by Derett's hand. He pressed his fingers against her lips, then lightly tapped them along the curve as she went still.

"Remember, I'm making every little thing about you my business," he whispered. With slow deliberation he drew his hand back to set his fingertips upon his own mouth. Then he wheeled and was gone.

Loy sputtered with indignation . . . and unwilling excitement.

The indignation faded first. All the way home her lips tingled where his fingers had lain. The thrill of his brief touch, his husked whisper, coursed like hotly flashing electricity through her veins. Her pulse charged wildly and her heart clamored above the traffic's noise. She throbbed from head to toe with a gnawing hunger. This was desire as she'd never experienced with Keith, had only imagined feeling with Stan. She wanted Derett Graham. Knowing *he* wanted *her* made her head spin and her stomach flutter.

She pulled into her garage, turned off the ignition, and sat tapping her leather key chain. As her keys rattled against the steering column, she prayed for sunny skies. The sooner she got Derett through his lessons, the better for her peace of mind!

CHAPTER FIVE

Her prayers were answered. The weather stayed cooperatively clear and calm, enabling them to fly each evening
without worry. More than ever, Cloud Sailing became the
focal point of Loy's existence. But for once it wasn't the
exhilaration of the flight that captivated her.

That, however, was one of the things Loy had shoved
to the back of her mind, shut in a compartment labeled To
Be Thought About Some Other Day.

She certainly refused to think about it tonight. She
leaned back against the wood of the trailer and looked out
over the empty soccer field. Not seeing either the rest of
her crew or her expected passengers, she checked her
watch. It was earlier than she'd thought and with an
impatient sigh—though just *why* she was so impatient was
one of the subjects stuck in that convenient mind-com-
partment of hers—Loy plopped down on the back end of
the trailer. She stretched her legs over the wood and
watched Gary fiddle with the CB. The channels hadn't
been working properly lately and he was trying to find the
problem. It was so odd, but for such a big man, with such
large hands, he had a feather-light touch. He could fix
almost anything. *Except,* thought Loy ruefully, *my
disobedient, willful, incredibly insane desires.*

Over the past two weeks Loy had found her resistance
to Derett fading. He was, on the one hand, too persistent
and too pleasant to ignore. On the other, he seemed to
have accepted her dictum of strictly business between

them and while he'd been determinedly friendly, he had not been one jot more intimate than that. Loy was no longer certain which bothered her the more: his continued attentiveness or his continued restraint.

The distant low growl of a motorcycle grew into a roar. The bike skidded to a halt beyond the edge of the playing field. Derett kicked the stand down and slid off the machine with the agility that marked all his movements. As he pulled off the scuffed royal blue helmet, Loy's heart began to thump alarmingly. He strolled forward with the self-assured step that was uniquely his, legs and hips moving fluidly, mesmerizing her as she watched him approach.

She dropped her eyes to her hands as he reached her side. When she flicked them back up, her gaze was teasingly perplexed. "Derett? Derett Graham?"

He smiled, tentatively, questioningly. "Yes. Or so I was the last time I checked."

"Are you sure?" She raised a hand to shade her eyes as she inspected him from head to toe. Her long hair swayed as she shook her head. "Well, you do look kinda like him, but, no, I don't think so."

"What sort of identification do you need, ma'am? A driver's license? Birth certificate? Ah, I know. I have the very proof." He put his hand to the etched silver buckle on his leather belt and began undoing it.

Loy stiffened. "What are you doing?"

"Trying to prove who I am." His hand dropped to his zipper. "I have a very unique birthmark on my—"

"That's okay! I believe you!"

"But I'd be happy to show you the birthmark. I don't get much opportunity to display it, since it's on my—"

"Unless it's shaped like a camera, I wouldn't believe it anyway," Loy interrupted quickly. She knew he'd been teasing, but her heart had nearly ceased operation just the same. "I just couldn't be too sure, you know. Without that damn camera slung over your shoulder, I almost didn't recognize you."

He laughed and rebuckled his belt. Easing down into place beside her, he explained. "I decided I was hauling dead weight around. I've realized a man can either crew or he can shoot, but he damned well can't do both."

The wind whisked a stream of her hair across her face. She gratefully busied herself with tugging it back into place while struggling to regain her composure. She told herself she really didn't want to get involved with him. Not really. No matter how appealing, how sexy, how desirable he was.

"Besides," he went on, "I've gotten plenty of photos of the ground operation. Just like I think I've gotten plenty of experience on the ground. When do I get to fly, cap'n?"

With some reluctance Loy answered, "Whenever you'd like. Since I'm booked pretty solidly in the evenings, we'll have to go up in the mornings—*early* mornings. For a dawn flight we usually meet at five thirty and try to get in the air by six thirty, seven at the latest."

"How about tomorrow morning?"

She glanced fleetingly at him, her eyes sliding away swiftly, but not before she had seen the warmth flash in his eyes, darkening the brown flecks and causing her breath to catch. "If you like. And if the weather's okay."

"Great. I can't think of a better way to see the sunrise." He stood, smiled, and ambled over to Gary.

An odd sensation raced over Loy's skin. Once again he'd managed to excite her without raising a fingertip. A look, a low husk to his tone, a suggestive smile—these were all he needed to make her heart flutter and her breath falter. Instead of growing more accustomed and therefore less susceptible to him, she'd become more and more hungry for him each passing day. It was why she hadn't wanted to start the flying lessons. Being aloft, alone together, seemed to her to be the epitome of exquisite torture.

The tinny blare of rock music blasted onto the scene as a rusted convertible screeched into place behind Derett's motorcycle. Roger and Danny vaulted over the side and swaggered across the field. "Sorry we're late," said Dan as they stopped before Loy. "But our car gave out and we had to hook a lift from some friends."

The music was already fading amid a squeal of tires as the convertible disappeared down the road.

"Yeah," grumbled Roger. "The bug gasped its last breath right on I-70 in the middle of rush hour."

"You want me to take a look at it?" asked Gary as he came up behind the trio.

"Nah. No real use. It was done for anyway." Roger kicked a clod of dirt at the trailer's back tire. "It's not even worth what it cost us to have it towed to the junkyard."

It was agreed that they'd had tough luck and, more, that they wouldn't be able to help with the morning flights. Dan explained that they probably wouldn't find any wheels until school was out and they couldn't count on anyone to drive them out before dawn.

Loy reassured Derett that with three people who knew what they were doing, there'd be no problem in getting aloft. "It's better, of course, when you have a crew of four or five, but three can do it. There have been times when Gary and I have managed by ourselves—with the inexperienced help of our terrified passengers."

She exchanged a fond, reminiscent smile with Gary, then happened to glance back at Derett. Her smile wilted. The next moment she blinked, uncertain that she had indeed seen a flash of fulminating fury in his gaze. He looked friendly enough now and even smiled. But, she realized as she turned toward the sound of an approaching vehicle, it was the smile without the dimples.

Derett's smile was forgotten in the flurry of greeting the newcomers, the charter for the evening. Two middle-aged men and their wives piled out of a station wagon, followed by a stream of kids of all shapes and sizes. As Loy talked to her passengers, and their wives hung back somewhat apologetically, the children swirled around Derett. Glancing in his direction, she saw two little girls each hanging on one of his arms, while a tow-headed boy rode happily on his shoulders. One of the mothers laughingly protested and remarked that, for a bachelor, he was unusually at ease with children. Loy would have known then, if he hadn't already told her so, that Derett came from a large family.

As spring moved toward summer she'd learned a lot about Derett Graham, more than she had wanted to, she privately thought. But any disinclination on her part to hear him out had been utterly disregarded by Derett. He'd told her how growing up as one of seven Air Force brats had been both interesting—he'd lived all over the world, in England, Hawaii, Germany, Texas, to name a few places—and instructive.

"I learned early on to be independent. With six others to compete with for attention at home, I had to speak up or get lost in the crowd, and with all the moving, I had to make friends quickly and easily or be left out of things."

"I think it sounds fabulous," she responded with just a hint of a wistful sigh. "I've lived in Kansas City all my life. I'd never even been out of Missouri until I married Keith and he took me to Colorado to ski. And my family's small—just my sister, Lisle, and me. I can't imagine what it would be like to have lived your kind of life."

He pondered this for a time, then shrugged. "I can't say I haven't been happy—I have—but growing up as I did has made it hard for me to put down roots in any one place. I've wandered and rambled and, all the while, I've envied people like you, people who had a hometown, who had friendships that lasted more than a year or two, who never had to say good-bye."

Looking at him now, Loy pushed memories away and set her mind on the flight ahead. The winds, perky all day long, had picked up, and though she didn't like to chance high-wind flights too often, tonight it suited her mood to be caught up in one. She wouldn't have time for any other, more dangerous, thoughts.

Because she was rushing to get aloft, she signaled her crew to release the tether ropes too soon. The balloon tried to respond to the heat she was shooting into it, but it wavered dangerously, not rising, just scudding forward. She saw Derett and Gary running toward the basket, saw her two male passengers eye the ground warily, as if measuring how far they had to jump to reach safety. She pressed down on the blast valve, sending a continuous hiss of heat upward. It lurched as though about to pitch over, then suddenly, miraculously, the balloon quavered and began climbing into the clouds.

Below her, sticklike figures waved and amplified shouts rose to reach them. As she maneuvered the balloon with accustomed ease, Loy's reflections unwillingly drifted once again to Derett.

Like herself, he'd fallen into his present career somewhat by accident. After graduating in Germany from Nuremberg American High School, he'd enrolled in college at the Munich campus of the University of Maryland. But his "wanderlust," as he put it, struck him during the second semester. He dropped out and starting hitching around the world. Along the way he picked up three languages and a camera.

His first work had been pretty much hit-and-miss—occasional shots sold to travel magazines. But then he'd ended up in a Turkish airport the night three young Americans were arrested for drug smuggling. He managed to sneak out a roll of film capturing the shock, the despair, the fright, of the three as the grim ordeal occurred and his journalistic career was begun. Without boasting, he'd explained how, over the years, he'd garnered steady assignments and a first-rate reputation, particularly for action work. She knew without his saying that it was because he gave the depth and feeling of experience to each shot, that he immersed himself in the action he photographed.

She only had to look at his fit physique to know that. She quickly glanced away from the sight.

"What made you decide to take a flight?" she asked, more to distract herself than to find out why.

He stood beside the Scout, amid the reddish glare of the convenience-store lights, and smiled up at her through the open window. "Impulse. I'd been in Kansas City exactly a week when I saw a balloon on the horizon and mentioned to a grocery clerk how terrific it would be to go up in one. Turned out he knew Gary. I called him the next day and arranged for a flight with Cloud Sailing." He leaned slightly toward her and let his smile slowly fade away. "It rather makes me believe in destiny."

He had walked away before she could do anything more than sputter. It was the way he left her all too often. Sputtering breathlessly while trying to rein in her stampeding desires.

In exchange for all his revelations about himself she'd spoken cautiously of her childhood and of her family. But of herself since high school she'd told him next to nothing. She intended to keep it that way. For the umpteenth time since she'd met him, Loy resolved not to make any more of a fool of herself than she already had.

They were chased by the station wagon as well as the Scout, with Derett's motorcycle strapped into the trailer. When they finally bounced to a standstill in a fairly easy landing, they were met by the same swarm of children that had seen them off. Loy tried to find something for the older ones to do while explaining what was going on. She handed out cans of soda pop and had just pulled the champagne from the cooler when Derett came around the side of the Scout to take it from her hands.

"I'll be right back," he said tersely and left. She didn't have time to wonder what he was doing before he returned empty-handed. "Gary's doing the ceremony," he said. He took her by the elbow and steered her away from everyone else. "Come on. I want to talk to you."

"Just where do you think you get off deciding who's to do what?" she inquired indignantly. "I'm in charge here, in case you'd forgotten."

She might as well have saved her breath. He took absolutely no notice of her anger, but hustled her beyond range of the group circling the vehicles. He didn't release her elbow until he jerked her to a stop. They stood facing each other across the dusty expanse of a one-lane country road.

"You'd better have a damn good explanation—" she began hotly.

"With all those kids around," he interrupted on a brusque bite, "I couldn't ask Gary. I didn't want to alarm anyone. Then several of the kids rode with us and I never got the chance to find out."

"What are you talking about?" A wave of total bewilderment submerged her annoyance.

"What happened on your takeoff? Were you in danger? When the damn thing wavered and looked like it was about to topple over, I swear my heart stopped working."

Her mouth opened, then closed. He looked at her with such obvious concern that she couldn't think of what to say. He grabbed her arm and jerked impatiently on it.

"Damn it, Loy! Tell me, were you in danger?"

"No—no, of course not," she was finally roused into saying. "I just tried to take off too soon, that's all. It's what we call false lift. The balloon wasn't hot enough to get out of the vacuum created by the winds, so I had to continually apply heat." He still looked thoroughly unconvinced. Without thinking, Loy reached out and gently touched his cheek. "I was fine, really."

He continued to stare, his eyes darkly intent. Her fingers trembled and fell back to her side. The air between them crackled with unspoken tension. Loy thought her heart might catapult out of her chest in the seconds that stretched silently by. Finally he said flatly, "I'll be at your place tomorrow at five thirty." Then he turned and strode away to mount his motorcycle.

73

Once again he left her speechless, breathless, and utterly disconcerted.

"You just flunked your first test as a pilot," said Loy with dry satisfaction.

"Oh?" Derett flicked his lashes down, unnerving her with the simple motion.

Everything about him unnerved her, damn him! The gondola had never seemed so small. Now it was so cramped, she felt she was suffocating. Each time he moved she felt the rustle of it; each time he breathed she heard the intake of it; each time he looked at her she saw the caress of it. Like now.

She averted her eyes, fastening them firmly on the metal burner above his head. His browned hand curled around the valve and she wondered fleetingly what the touch of that hand would be like. Strong and sure? Gentle? Eager? Her heart gave an odd kick and she thrust her unwanted suppositions aside.

"When you apply heat, you must look up, into the balloon," she said with a tinge of asperity. "Otherwise you could tilt the burner on its springs and burn a hole in the fabric. Which at forty-five bucks a panel—or more—could get pretty costly."

"Aye, aye, cap'n," he said cheerfully, and pressed on the blast valve again, this time tipping his head slightly to follow the upward streak of flame with his gaze.

In those fractional moments Loy observed him openly, as she'd secretly longed to do all morning. The first rays of sunlight laced through his hair like antique gold, muted yet glowing. It bronzed the skin of his bare arms, the arched column of his neck, the strong structure of his face. Though his dimples were nowhere in sight, Loy was certain she knew just where they'd next appear.

He released the valve and glanced at her, his green eyes glinting knowingly. Embarrassed, she quickly looked away, gazing at the patchwork of shadow and light on the earth below.

"How was that?"

"Fine." She paused. He was staring at her. In an attempt to distract him, she rushed into speech. "A friend of mine did that once. Burned a hole in his balloon. He—Bob Coulter—has been flying for more than a decade, but just once he paid more attention to the action below than to the burner, tipped it, and cost himself eleven thousand dollars."

Derett whistled. "Expensive mistake."

"One he hasn't made again, I assure you," she responded, while trying to ignore the way in which the purse of his lips gave them a sensual fullness not normally visible.

"No one can afford to make such mistakes twice," he commented, capturing Loy's attention from the curve of his mouth.

Her smile slid off her face. "No, they can't," she agreed shortly.

Turning her gaze to the Kansas countryside over which they were flying, she experienced a wave of self-reproach. She should know all about mistakes. She was the type of fool who'd made the same one twice before learning. She would not, could not, be crazy enough to do so again!

"You ever do that?"

Loy jumped, misunderstanding for one second what he meant. Surely he hadn't read her mind! Then, realizing she was being an absolute idiot, she forced herself to answer calmly. "Burned my balloon? No, not like that, though like everyone else, I've put small holes into the envelope. But I've done plenty of other stupid things over the years —we all do—including several bone-rattling landings."

There was an appraising gleam in Derett's eyes that told her he sensed how much the undercurrent of the conversation disturbed her. She feared he would pursue it, but he earned her gratitude by pointing to the west and saying, "Look at that. We're being chased by our shadow."

The clear outline of the balloon followed them on the horizon, gliding silently over clumps of trees and flowing wheatfields. Though there was little sensation of gaining ground, the floating silhouette marked their progress as they skimmed high over farm rooftops. The noise of the burner spooked a herd of cows. With lolling squeals they stampeded in a puff of dust. As the balloon rose, moving faster as it gained altitude, Derett released the valve and the cattle quietly returned to their grazing. Loy squinted down at the dust settling around the calming herd. A breeze gently caressed her skin, warmed by the burner's heat, and she inhaled the fresh air with a feeling of gladness.

Between whooshes of the burner they began to talk lightly, easily, like old friends. Loy related several humorous incidents from her first flights and found herself laughing with him. She knew sharing laughter with him was nearly as dangerous as sharing intimate embraces. She knew, but she couldn't help herself. It was a perfect day for sharing, for being among the wisping clouds with laughter. The morning was gloriously golden, the sky beguilingly blue, and the man beside her heartstoppingly handsome.

She privately thought Derett was going to make an excellent pilot. He once noted the shift in wind, something natural pilots instinctively had a feel for, and several times he tapped the burner valve before she instructed him to do so. He leaned against the suede rim of the wicker, appearing deceptively relaxed, but she saw the taut readiness in his stance and knew he was alert. Yes, he'd make a good pilot.

For the landing, however, Loy once again took control. With a congenial smile she explained, "Until you're a little more practiced, I'd better handle the touchdowns, especially on the morning flights."

"Why especially in the mornings?" he queried.

"In the mornings the wind rises, so you generally have

calm takeoffs and windy landings. For evening flights the opposite is true. The wind dies, so your liftoffs are windy and your touchdowns are relatively calm."

He tipped his head slightly to the side, studying her. "I guess I'd noticed that last night when you came down so lightly after that godawful liftoff."

At the mention of last night, Loy hit the valve, silencing conversation with a heated hiss. She certainly didn't want to bring up his strange behavior of the night before. Things between them were nerve-wracking enough as it was.

The sun was fully risen; the world below coming to life with the first muted rumbles of traffic. A large brown mutt dashed out from a grove of trees to bark wildly, then raced back to his shelter. As the dog charged a second time they exchanged a smile. Brown flecks sparked within Derett's green eyes and warmed the tenor of his smile, making it an oddly intimate smile, a smile of lovers.

With effort Loy pulled away from the magnetism of the moment. She knew she must not permit him to smile at her like that. Becoming utterly businesslike, she explained her actions as she lowered the craft, using frequent short bursts of heat to control the rate of descent. Just as they jolted onto the grassy expanse of an open field, they heard the merry trumpeting of the Scout's horn announcing Gary's arrival. The basket dragged briefly as Loy tugged on the rip line to release the air from the balloon, then creaked to a halt.

Their first flight lesson was over.

They again smiled at one another. Derett's dimples made their appearance right where Loy had known they would. They mellowed the harsh planes of his face and unsettled her pulse. Damn, he'd done it again. Without a word to him she climbed out of the gondola and strode toward the crown of the envelope. Just a little longer and she'd be free of him for the day. Free from having to restrain her disobedient heart, her careening pulses.

But without Roger or Danny the packing up took longer than usual. Every minute was a delicious torment for Loy. She could not stop her gaze from following the fluid motion of Derett as he rolled the envelope, taped the lines, lifted the basket into the trailer. The cords in his arms stretched, then slackened, then stretched again in a hypnotic rhythm. His jeans rode low on his hips, tightly hugging the curve of his buttocks and molding the shape of his long legs. She was absorbed in his physical vitality, entranced by his simplest movement. She resented his masculine allure, yet at the same time she was grateful he was so well conditioned. She'd have him pilot-trained in a fingersnap's time. Or so she vowed to herself even as her eyes strayed back to him.

Before they parted that morning she presented Derett with one of her loveliest smiles. "You really did a great job for the first time up. You're an absolute natural. We'll have you licensed and on your own in no time."

As she drove away she stifled any desire to have it otherwise. It was the way it had to be and she told herself that was the way she wanted it.

The next two lessons, however, did not go as smoothly and Loy began to wonder if she'd been wrong in her initial assessment of Derett's abilities. He continually made little errors, seemingly forgetting her instructions the second she issued them. Worse, he couldn't seem to judge when to shift direction, when to catch the wind current to carry the balloon toward a specific spot. She patiently explained how to gain or lose altitude to catch a directional current, then explained yet again. Usually Loy had no difficulty retaining her patience with a student. Usually she did not expect students to sense the vagaries of the wind. Usually. This time she wanted her student to learn instantly, to get over the lessons and out of her life as swiftly as possible.

By the end of the third flight, when Derett again asked how to take the balloon to the left, Loy's patience shattered. She glared at him and bit out through clenched teeth, "You want to go left? Jump out and walk there!"

"I'm just trying to understand—" he began blandly.

"That isn't something I can teach you! A pilot has to be able to sense these things! It's a feel, a skill, to ride the winds." Loy stopped to grab a breath and realized to her horror that she'd been yelling. She took another, deeper, more calming breath. "I'm sorry. I didn't mean to lose my temper. Don't worry, Derett, it'll come to you."

"That's okay." He turned slightly, gazing out over the city park they were passing.

Loy looked at him sharply. He'd sounded boyishly hurt. Too hurt. Sudden suspicions rose like hackles bristling. Was he playing at being dumb? But why? "You're doing fine, really," she said evenly. "By the time you log in your tenth hour, you'll have all that it takes to be a pilot."

"What if I don't?"

"You will."

"But if I don't," he persisted, meeting her probing gaze with a look of concern, "then what? Do we log in more hours?"

Loy studied him from beneath lowered lashes, noting the shrewd deliberation in his eye. She offered a tight smile. "I doubt that will be necessary."

"I hope you're right," he said, jerking on the valve.

"Look up!" she shouted above the deafening noise. She frowned at him, but she was no longer angry. She was puzzled. He was stalling, she was certain of it. He was too sharp not to remember such little things as watching the valve as you hit it. The question was, why? And what should she do about it?

At the same time Loy asked herself why she should care if he prolonged the lessons. After all, she reasoned with herself, she was being well paid for her time. The longer he took, the more she made. So why should she care if he was stalling?

But Loy did care and she knew it. The more she saw of him, the more her resistance to him eroded. She felt a trembling thrill simply being near him. Unfortunately she knew what kind of pain and heartache that sort of thrill led to. Derett was dangerous to her emotional health and she really couldn't let him go on playing dumb this way.

But she was strangely reluctant to accuse him.

CHAPTER SIX

An iridescent prism spanned the glowing dawn, arching over bulbous treetops to fade gently from view. The distinct outline of a balloon traversed the bridge of the rainbow. It seemed to pause a moment at the apex of the colorful curve, then skimmed silently onward.

Loy glanced at Derett beside her and breathed in an awed whisper, "Riding a rainbow's supposed to be good luck . . . I've never done it before."

He leaned toward her, his scent and warmth touching her. Caressing her cheek with his breath, he murmured, "That's because you've been waiting for me. It's *our* good luck, Loy. It's for our future."

The words lingered in the air as radiant as the rainbow, as warm as the morning sun.

With a force of will she hadn't suspected she possessed, Loy stepped away from the searing intimacy, shrugging it away. "Good luck for our lessons," she said with credible ease.

"Good luck for us," he repeated.

Despite her firm resolution not to care what he said or did, her pulse instantly accelerated to the speed of sound. She braced against the suede-covered upright and gazed out over the horizon. She didn't want to take note of Derett as he guided the balloon. She didn't want to see how his muscles worked in fluid rhythm with each little move he made, how his lashes flicked whenever he glanced her way, how his dimples creased the tawny surface beside his mouth as he smiled lazily. And she especially didn't want to see his green eyes glitter darkly as they settled on her. Not that it seemed to mean anything anyway.

No matter how often, how intensely, his gaze lingered on her, Derett had not made a single attempt to change the tenor of their relationship. Oh, he made occasional remarks that could only be labeled as suggestive and he certainly took advantage of every opportunity to disconcert her with brief, glancing touches. But he had not attempted anything more. He hadn't even asked her out for so much as a drink.

Loy knew she should be relieved, thankful, accepting. She wasn't. She was bothered by his tactics. Why didn't he carry through with what his eyes told her he wanted? She kept her attention fixed on the passing scenery and told herself she didn't care, she did not care. Not in the least.

Between the houses and trees gliding by below ran a ribbon of paved road. She saw the red and white Scout in the distance, hovering at an intersection, then turn right, following them by sight. They'd failed to raise Gary on the radio earlier and could only hope they'd stay in his view.

As if he read her mind, Derett voiced her thought. "Should we try the CB again?"

Shaking her head, she replied, "I don't think there's any use in trying it. Unless he seems to lose sight of us, I don't think we have to worry."

"Lose sight of us? Loy, we're bigger than some houses and much more colorful. How could he lose track of us?"

"I know it seems like it would be impossible to lose sight of something this obvious, but believe me, it isn't." She wrapped her fingers into her hair and looked away from his teasing eyes. "It's particularly easy on hazy days, but even on clear days like today it can happen. Especially out in the country like this, where so many roads twist and bend and end up a dead end. All it takes is a fast wind or a clump of trees or buildings to obscure the chaser's view and bingo! We're lost."

He laughed and all of a sudden Loy found that the gondola was unbearably crowded. She untwined the flaxen hair from her fingers and said somewhat hastily, "Speaking of wind, do you feel how it's increasing? I think perhaps we'd better land before we're blown into Oz."

"You're the captain," he promptly agreed.

"Okay, mate, it's about time to see if you can handle the landing of this ship."

"Do you think I'm ready for that?" he queried, slanting a doubtful look at her.

"Let's see, shall we?" she replied with a tight smile.

He hesitated, wearing a mien of uncertainty that she silently labeled as phony as a three-dollar bill. As if he'd ever had moment of doubt in his life! She stretched out her long arm and pointed. "That field over there looks good. Go for it."

Although the morning had been relatively calm, winds had risen briskly as they flew over the southeast countryside. Derett misjudged the current's force and descended too rapidly. The basket hit the ground with too much speed. At the first teeth-jarring impact he pulled the rip line. The wind grabbed hold of the balloon and they plowed across the tall grass under full, billowing sail. They bounced within the basket like apples bobbing in a bucket. The wind abruptly released its furious grip and without warning the basket crashed on its side.

As they toppled Derett pulled Loy into his arms, attempting to shelter her from both the hard ground and the heavy propane tanks with the length of his body. "Are you all right?" he asked when the wicker had finally ceased to rock.

"I—yes," huffed Loy. She lay within his hold, simply trying to regain the breath that had been knocked from her.

"Did I rattle your bones?"

She couldn't help responding to the laughter in his voice. With a breathless chuckle she nodded. "Like casta-nets. If you were trying to rattle my bones, Graham, you've done a class-A job of it."

His eyes searched her face, then abruptly closed. "Oh, I just got what I've been wanting to do to your bones," he said lightly. Then he lifted his lids and the passion darken-ing his eyes stole all Loy's recovered breath.

For a suspended moment their gazes held. The ropes and wicker creaked like a ship asea. Unseen insects whirred and droned. Leaves rustled in the wind. The wild beat of Loy's heart deafened her to them all.

She suddenly realized his full weight pressed upon her. Her breasts were flattened by his chest, her hips were ground against his groin, her legs were tangled with his as only lovers' should be. His silver buckle bit into the soft-ness of her stomach; his blue jeans scratched the length of her bare legs. But Loy didn't notice her discomfort. She was aware of only one thing.

His mouth poised a breath away from hers.

As if of their own volition, her eyelids dropped, her lips parted in anticipation of his kiss. The heat of his breath tantalized her waiting mouth. Then he nestled his lips in the dishevelment of her hair and he whispered hoarsely, "From the moment I saw you, I've been wanting to jump on your bones."

With a husky laugh he rolled away and rose in one swift motion. Loy's eyes flew open and she gawked in disbelief as he stood gazing down at where she was still sprawled. She saw the teasing laughter threaded through the dark desire in his eyes and regret surged through her. It was a fierce, tumultuous flood of gut-level, aching need. As she stared upward the humor passed from his gaze, leaving only an overwhelming intensity.

Loy was the first to pull her eyes away. She had to. She scrambled to her feet and looked beyond the crumpled balloon, the tipped-over gondola. Studying the semi-circle of trees bounding them to the left, she murmured unsteadily, "Where are we?"

The field they'd landed in was, like many skirting the city, an isolated rural isle. Tall prairie grass rippled amidst a concert of humming insects. A wire fence extended into the trees and beyond, but the field was open to the right. There wasn't a building or a road to be seen, though Loy remembered seeing a road just past the trees.

Kneeling beside the basket, she picked up the CB radio. "Sixteen to Cloud Chaser. Come in Chaser." Static crackled back. "Sixteen to Cloud Chaser." Again only the crackling silence responded. They eyed each other over the radio, then Loy stood to shove it into Derett's hand. "Damn this thing. I'll either have to get it fixed or replaced. For now, keep trying to reach them while I start on the envelope."

After several more unsuccessful attempts to reach Gary, he gave it up and began helping Loy roll up the balloon. The gaseous odor of heated fabric filled their nostrils and bugs buzzed past them as they worked side by side. They did not speak.

Derett unhooked the steel lines and handed them to Loy, who taped them together. Once, their fingertips grazed and both jerked back. Their eyes met, then slid swiftly away. This was, thought Loy as she wrapped the masking tape over the lines, pure hell. If Gary didn't put in an appearance soon, she was going to give vent to a blood-curdling scream.

They were packing the envelope into the canvas sleeve when an abrupt, distinct horn blared nearby. Loy raced to the basket, retrieved the radio and breathlessly called, "Sixteen to Cloud Chaser."

There was a fragmentized click, then Gary's calm voice. "You got Chaser here. Where the hell are you?"

"Good question. The horn sounds loud and clear. We're in a grassy field beyond the barricade of trees which I hope you can see from wherever you are."

"Right ho. See ya soon."

She and Derett had the uprights and instrument panel removed and were just about to try the CB again when the Scout rolled into view, cutting straight through the trees toward them.

"You two okay?" asked Gary as he lumbered up to them. "That was some descent. You practically free-fell to the ground."

Loy assured him that they'd suffered nothing more than a few possible bruises and Derett adjoined that his ego was bruised more than anything else. They then efficiently finished packing and loading up. Though it had become routine for Derett to ride up front with Loy on the way home, nothing was said when he climbed into the trailer. Nor did Gary ask any questions during the long ride back to the convenience store. Instead, he fixed his brown eyes on the road and waited patiently for Loy to break the strained silence.

She couldn't. The memory of the warmth of Derett's breath hovering over her lips still burned her. She would have kissed him then, ardently, without restraint, without a thought to the consequences. And instead of thanking her lucky stars for her narrow escape from those consequences, she was aching with the need to understand what had happened. *Why* hadn't he taken the kiss she so freely offered? Why?

There was no charter scheduled for that night, for which Loy could only be grateful. She was certain the last thing she would be able to endure was another disturbing encounter with Derett.

Once a month John and Esther McDaniel had their daughters over for a family dinner. It was generally a happy gathering, Lisle's children being spoiled by their cheery grandmother while John and Bill Craeger dissected the latest sports events and the sisters settled down for a long exchange of gossip. This night, however, Lisle pressed Loy for "all the juicy details" of her sessions with Derett Graham. Having the tenacity of a bulldozer, Lisle extracted far more than Loy had been willing to tell and long before Esther carried the roast beef to the table, Loy had a massive headache.

Over a meal that Loy couldn't taste, Lisle regaled them all with the tale of the Dom Pérignon, leading her parents and even Bill to evidence an unusual interest in Loy's current ballooning student. Their probing and prying, though kindly meant, grated on her nerves. It was all she could do to remain barely civil. As soon as the last plate had been cleared from the table, Loy bid her family good night and took her headache home.

Once there, she fixed a cup of herb tea and sat in the living room, pouring out all her troubles between sips to an inattentive Jeeves. Though she was feeling out of sorts with her family, she was, she told the sleeping lump of fur at her feet, even more so with a certain photojournalist. Her sister's teasing had simply compounded what she viewed as Derett's sins.

She had to face facts. The fact was Derett Graham was encroaching on her hard-won independence. She could no longer ignore the fact that seeing him had become the highlight of her day, nor that seeing him plucked her nerves like tensed strings. Worse, she was beginning to *like* the jittery way she felt around him. She set down her teacup and complained aloud, "He's disrupting my life!"

Jeeves issued a heavy snore, but no solutions. With a disheartened sigh Loy went to bed, feeling unjustly abused. Waking from a restless night of tossed sleep, she left the house in what could only be described as a grumpy frame of mind. In the dim shadows of the convenience-store parking lot, the first thing she saw through the swirling morning haze was the source of all her distressed dreams.

He lounged on his motorcycle with a container of coffee in his hand, wearing jeans so faded they shone as gray as the mist furling about his long legs. His plain black T-shirt stretched over his solidly muscled chest and his belt buckle glinted against a firm, flat stomach. He looked lean and assured and sexy as hell. Loy ignored him.

Slamming to a jerking halt, she slid out of the Scout and strode to the phone to call flight service. The report of a front on the way should have pleased her. Now she wouldn't have to suffer Derett's company. It didn't please her. It depressed her, leaving her more annoyed than ever. She trudged back to where Gary now stood yawning sleepily beside Derett.

"We can't go up. Winds are at thirteen miles per hour and visibility is marginal at best, maybe five miles. It won't get better; they say a storm front's moving in. So, I'll thank you both for getting up and ask you to call me this afternoon if conditions have improved."

She whirled, her long braid swishing through the air as she did so. After two steps she realized Derett was beside her. She stopped and slid her gaze over him. "Yes?"

"Don't you owe me something?"

"Owe you?" Loy's fair brows shot up in astonishment.

"The lesson."

"Didn't you hear what I just said? We can't go up." She paused, looking away from the appeal in his eyes, then added in a calmer tone, "Look, it's an old adage among balloonists that I'd rather be on the ground wishing I were flying than in the air wishing I were on the ground."

His melodious chuckle tore at her. "And so would I."

"Good. We'll fly tomorrow." She nodded a dismissal and walked on. Derett walked with her. Again she halted. This time she faced him directly. "Was there something else?" she inquired in tones thick with frost.

"There's still the lesson you owe me."

She had to be grateful her jaw was hinged into place. Otherwise she knew her chin would have dropped completely off. She pulled it back into place with an audible snap. "Didn't we just go over this? Didn't I just tell you we can't fly this morning and didn't you just say you'd rather stay on the ground?"

"Yes," he agreed, smiling.

"Good. I'm glad we agree on it." She didn't even take so much as a step this time. He reached out and curled his hand over her arm, anchoring her in place.

"But I'm still paying for the time. Nothing was said about lessons being conducted strictly in the air. I figured you could answer some questions for me."

Loy knew she should refuse and go home. But her eyes riveted on the frayed fabric along the zipper of his jeans and she couldn't stop staring, couldn't think of anything to say. She had the insane compulsion to run her finger over the frayed denim. She heard him breathe her name and wrenched her eyes upward. "W-what sort of questions?" she stuttered, not caring.

"I'm still not clear about the qualifying system for the Nationals, for one thing. How points are awarded, for another," he replied as he crumpled his coffee container and sent it sailing through the haze toward the trash barrel standing some feet away.

"Oh. Well, for every event sanctioned," she began.

"We can't talk here," he interrupted decisively. "Come on, help me strap my motorcycle into your trailer."

Realizing he was walking away, she opened the back end of her wooden trailer and stumbled after him, protesting, "But where would we go?"

"Your place, my place, who cares? As long as we're out of this mist. It's damn chilly for the first of June, don't you think?" His dimples dented beside a coaxing smile and Loy found herself helping him lift, then strap, his bike to the siderail of her trailer.

Seated beside him, her hand poised over her keys, Loy asked in a neutral voice, "Where do you live?" She didn't want him invading her territory any more than he'd already done. This would be strictly business, she silently reaffirmed even as her heart threatened to kick down her rib cage.

He gave precise, concise directions and as Loy turned east to drive into Missouri, he sprawled, as he had before, as if he owned the seat. Didn't he ever just sit? Did he always take casual possession like this? She was certain he did and her nerves capered at the thought.

"How was your night off? Do anything special?" he queried in a friendly way.

"Ummm," she answered.

A small silence lasted until they crossed State Line Road. Then Derett shifted, bending his leg onto the seat and resting his knee just a hairline from her thigh. Her heart went into overtime, pumping blood that racketed through her veins. She could feel the erratic flutter of her pulse as she tried not to notice the knee, the muscled thigh, the man.

"Have a big date?" he asked casually.

"Oh!" Loy nearly hopped an inch off the seat at the unexpectedness of it. Cracking her mouth in a caricature of a smile, she shook her head, swishing her long plait. "No. I spent the evening with my family. My folks have my sister and me over for a big dinner once a month. Mother seems to think it's the only way she can be sure we're eating properly. She stuffs us so full in one night, it takes the rest of the month to digest it."

As she spoke Loy calmed. Her pulse stopped racing as her heart resumed a steady beat. *You're being an ass, Loy McDaniel,* she told herself sternly. *Anyone would think you'd never seen a man's knee.* He inquired about her sister and she happily told him the history of Lisle's life.

When Loy arrived at Derett's home she had to stifle exclamations of surprise. She'd have thought—if she'd thought about his life at all, which she firmly refused to do—that he was the type to live in a sterile, contemporary block of apartments. Certainly not a rambling, three-story

Dutch colonial house set in a tree-lined neighborhood that epitomized mid-American ideals.

Inside, her preconceptions received an even bigger jolt. The spacious, old-fashioned rooms were at once both comfortable and stylish. Before turning into the living room, she peeked at the dining room and was astounded to see warm deep-red walls. The room, however, didn't appear the least closed in. The clear glass dining table and open latticework shutters on the windows gave it an airy feeling. The living room was just as lovely. Two plump rust-colored sofas faced each other across the expanse of a richly worked Oriental rug and fairly begged to be lounged on. To the left of the sofas was a fireplace with a gleaming darkwood mantel, and to the right sat a pair of equally plump and inviting armchairs. Loy perched gingerly on the edge of one and eyed Derett warily.

"You like it?" he asked, standing by the door.

"Very much," she confessed reluctantly. "It's . . . not what I expected."

The dimples came and went in a flash. "Would you like something to drink? Coffee? Tea?" He paused, rubbed his foot along his calf, and raised his brows suggestively. "Or me?"

"Coffee will be fine, thank you," she said tersely.

He took a step, stopped, and bent to vigorously scratch at both his legs. When he looked up he caught Loy watching him and explained, "Chiggers. I got eaten alive in that field yesterday."

She couldn't repress a laugh. He looked comical, standing like a stork sliding his foot along his leg. He frowned at her and she rose. "Have you put anything on the bites?"

"I've tried every spray I could find and nothing's helped." His frown deepened and his gaze turned accusatory. "Why weren't you bitten? You were wearing shorts!"

"I always put on a repellent before flying," she answered smugly. Relenting, she offered him a soft smile. "I

91

think I've got something that will take care of your bites. You go get that coffee and I'll be right back."

She found what she wanted in the Scout's glove compartment and returned to await Derett in his living room. On either side of the fireplace books and miscellany crowded floor-to-ceiling shelves. She wandered over and examined titles, again suppressing her surprise at seeing worn and obviously well-read copies of *War and Peace, Tom Jones,* and *Great Expectations* leaning against each other. Not for the world would Loy have revealed that these were among her own often-read favorites. She turned away from the discovery of shared tastes. She didn't want to share anything with Derett Graham!

The glint of a square brass picture frame standing on the mantelpiece caught her eye and she reached for it. Her hand remained motionless an inch from the brass as she realized who it was captured within that frame.

She was leaning on the railing of Coulter's trailer, her hair rippling in the breeze, her lips parted in laughter. Looking at the photo, Loy remembered the moment. She'd heard the click and turned to see him pointing his camera at her. She remembered her surge of fear and rage and wished desperately she could feel them now. What she felt was a quivering that began in her toes and sent exciting tingles all the way up to her head.

"It's a great shot, isn't it?"

Loy swung round to see Derett standing in the doorway, holding two lemon-yellow ceramic mugs and grinning widely at her. Some of her anger returned at his cocky satisfaction. "You had no right to take those pictures," she said. She sounded sulky; she knew it and she resented it.

He grinned more broadly and sauntered forward. "How could I resist? You're very photogenic. If you weren't a pilot, you could be a model. It's not fair to expect a photographer to pass up taking photos of you."

She gave up the argument. It only provided him the

opportunity to be more appealing than ever and she didn't need that. Taking the mug he held out to her, she ordered, "Roll up your jeans."

With great deliberation Derett held her gaze as he slowly sipped his coffee, then set the mug on the mantel beside the brass frame. "Perhaps I should take them off," he drawled provocatively. "I have bites all the way up to my—"

"That won't be necessary!" she cut in quickly.

"All the way up to my birthmark," he finished on a grin.

She set her own mug down with a heavy thump, sloshing coffee indiscriminately over the polished wood. Ignoring his low chuckle, she knelt on the deep pile of the rug and as he finished rolling the denim above his knees, she pursed her lips. "You weren't kidding, were you? You must have provided dinner for dozens of the little monsters."

His legs were covered with red bumps, many of which had obviously been aggravated by scratching. But Loy saw only the tantalizing beauty of those muscular legs. Hair as fine as gold dust covered the tanned length of them. A warm, clean, masculine scent filled her nostrils as Loy leaned closer to begin dabbing a clear liquid on the bites. She hoped he couldn't sense the trembling in her fingers.

"Hey, that stings! What the hell is it?"

She tilted back her head to gaze up at him. His protest had been friendly; his eyes as he looked down at her were even more so. Loy felt ridiculously subservient on her knees before him. She focused on a particularly large, ugly bump and sniped crossly, "It's clear fingernail polish and it stings because you've been scratching and opened the wounds."

"Well, what are you supposed to do with bites? They itched."

"You should ignore them. And you probably showered

93

or bathed in hot water when any fool knows that makes chigger bites worse."

"This fool didn't know it," he rejoined in a voice so full of warmth the end of Loy's nerves were burned.

She refused to look back up at him. She hurriedly coated all the bites, speaking only to direct him to turn around. Then she recapped the polish and stood. She drew in a long breath as she rose, feeling rather as if she'd been smothering.

"Are you so good at ignoring what bothers you?" asked Derett before she could step away from him.

A palpable heat charged the short space between them. It was stifling, yet oddly invigorating. Desire sparked the brown flecks in Derett's eyes as they fastened on the full curve of her mouth. Loy did not, as she thought she should, try to break away from the captivation of his heavy-lidded gaze. She was certain he was going to sweep her into his arms and a tremor of excitement overpowered her caution, her fear, her good sense. Her lashes dropped, her lips parted in breathy invitation.

Time hung suspended as Loy swayed dizzily. The warm caress of his breath stroked the edge of her quivering mouth. Then with a rustle, he moved away.

"Thanks for the ministrations, Nightingale," he said as he bent to roll his jean legs back into place.

Loy could only hope her face wasn't revealing her shocked chagrin. She felt like a fool. She'd once again misread his intentions and though she knew she should be relieved, she wasn't. Not in the least. She felt furious—and frustrated.

Clapping the nail polish onto the mantel, she said coldly, "Here. You keep this. I really must be going now. Thanks for the coffee."

Derett compounded his boorish behavior by not making the slightest attempt to detain her. He ushered her to the door with undo haste and said only mildly that he hoped the weather cleared by that evening so she could take up her charter.

It was only as she pulled into her drive that Loy realized he'd never asked her a single question regarding ballooning.

CHAPTER SEVEN

The shriek of the alarm was muffled beneath a reverberating crack of thunder. Loy snapped awake and bolted upright as she opened her eyes. Lightning danced beyond the rattling windowpane, briefly illuminating the interior of her bedroom. Even as darkness reclaimed the room, she glanced toward the nightstand where the alarm clock shrilled. The glowing numerals screamed the early hour. With a curse she jammed the button, then slid down onto her pillow into silence broken only by the heavy thrust of thundering rain against the house.

Rolling first to one side, then to the other, Loy knew she'd be unable to get back to sleep. She also knew there was no reason for her to get up. There'd be no flight this morning. She didn't want to acknowledge the wave of disappointment flooding her, but nothing could still the intensity of her regret.

These early morning flights alone with Derett had come to mean more than Loy cared to admit. She burrowed into the depths of her pillow, but it did no good. She failed to dispel the image of Derett tempting her with his crooked smile, tantalizing her with his melodious laughter, tormenting her with his brief, thrilling touch. He was, quite simply, driving her mad.

He wanted her. She knew it by the undisguised desire in his eyes whenever they fell on her. She knew it by the catch in his breath whenever their hands accidentally met. She knew it by the tingling of her own body in response to each rippling movement of his. And still he did nothing to take her.

After tossing restlessly for several more minutes, she sat up with a groan. Damn him! Each flight, each minute together made it harder for her to ignore what her body clamored for. Yesterday's fiasco at his home had been the worst. Twice now she had literally offered herself to him. Twice he had ignored the offer.

With yet another half-groan, half-sigh, Loy acknowledged that his rejection hurt. She ached with the bruising pain of it. She ached with wanting him.

She wanted him, wanted him, wanted him.

The litany drummed in her head until, with an irritated jerk, she swept herself up from the bed. She threw on a full-length cotton robe, belted it at the waist, and stumbled into the bathroom. But there was no escape from her thoughts. They haunted her dreams and hounded her days.

Brushing her teeth, she envisioned the morning they'd ridden the rainbow. She remembered the crash landing, the jolting and bouncing, and the sudden stillness. She felt again the weight of him pressed against her, the scrape of his denims over her legs, the mingling of his breath with hers. She tasted the kiss that had never been.

Realizing she was staring into the reflection of her widened gaze, visualizing a kiss she'd never received, Loy muttered a soft string of oaths. She rinsed her toothbrush vigorously, splattering the mirror, then flung it down and fled.

In the cheery brightness of the kitchen she filled her drip coffeemaker to the top. She had a feeling she'd need all ten cups this morning. While it was brewing she peered out her front window, trying to spot the newspaper through the continuing torrent of rain. In the end she gave up. It was probably ruined anyway. Back in the kitchen with Jeeves happily padding behind her, she settled down to her first cup with a grateful sigh.

That was when the doorbell rang.

Wisps of steam wafted from her coffee as Loy held it poised before her lips. A thunderclap was followed immediately by another impatient, imperious ring of the bell. She realized she hadn't imagined it and raced down the short steps, certain it must be a family emergency. Why else would anyone be out in a thunderstorm at this hour of the morning? Heart pumping furiously, she threw open the door.

A shapeless gray canvas slicker entered the foyer and Loy stepped back, suddenly frightened. Her legs buckled against a solid mound of fluffy fur behind her; simultaneously, Jeeves yipped loudly and Loy tumbled backward. She was rescued by a firm hand that shot from beneath the heavy canvas folds, clutching her arm and dripping water down her robe.

"Stop howling, Jeeves, or we'll throw you out into the rain," commanded Derett with laughter.

"You!" Relief gave way to exasperation. He'd scared the life out of her!

"You were expecting someone else?" He shoved the hood away from his face, revealing the rain-streaked glow of his skin, the crooked slant of his scarred eyebrow.

"Of course not. But I certainly wasn't expecting you either. What are you doing here?"

Handing her a waterlogged roll of newspaper, topped by his sodden slicker, Derett knelt to remove his equally wet shoes. He took his time in pulling them off, further incensing an already nervously furious Loy. "It was my understanding that we had an appointment this morning."

"You've got to be kidding! Surely you don't expect us to fly in this storm."

"No," he replied easily as he rose and smiled down at her. His gaze lingered on the rapid rise and fall of her breasts, then lifted to her flushed face. "But I thought we could have breakfast together and talk."

"Breakfast? But—" Loy stopped, then sighed. "I know, I know. You're paying for the lesson time."

"I wasn't exactly thinking of lessons, at least not in ballooning," he said in a low, husky voice that sent shivers down her spine. His lashes flicked once, then suddenly the easygoing, friendly Derett replaced the dangerously provocative man of a moment before. "You wouldn't want to send me back out in that storm, would you?"

Loy's mouth worked soundlessly for several seconds. Then, feeling water spattering on her bare toes, she discarded the ruined paper and clenched her fists over the canvas. Without so much as glancing at him, she strode off to the bathroom. Draping the hood over the showerhead so that the garment would drip into the tub, she muttered half-hearted oaths, promising she'd have him out the door before the slicker dried.

All the while Loy fought the excitement rising within her, crashing fiercely through her veins like a raging bull. She fought the intoxication of knowing that he had come, he was here with her.

She started back for the kitchen, but stopped abruptly as she realized her robe was clinging to her skin. The thin, damp cotton revealed more than it concealed. With yet another muffled curse, Loy wheeled around and darted into her bedroom.

A quarter-hour later she emerged, respectably attired in lilac slacks and a white scoop-necked blouse gaily embroidered along the bodice. The cotton slacks were loose and flowing, the peasant blouse cool and summery. Together they were casually seductive. But, of course, Loy had chosen the outfit for comfort and nothing else.

She had hurriedly piled her hair on top of her head, where it threatened to topple from the precarious confines of a tortoiseshell skewer. Nor had she taken the time for makeup, but there lay a glitter in the depths of her sea blue eyes that no clever application of cosmetics could have enhanced. Even as she told herself she wouldn't be taken in by any more of his tricks, hot anticipation galloped through her.

The pleasant timbre of his voice reached her before she entered the kitchen, harmonizing with a low, steady growl of pleasure. "Come on, gimme five. That's it. That's a boy. Here you go," she heard as she peered around the doorjamb. She saw Derett slip Jeeves a crunchy treat while ruffling his floppy ears. It was a happy scene. Homey. Loy moved to break it up.

"Coffee?" The query was as cool as Loy could make it, but Derett did not seem to notice her lack of warmth. He smiled and gestured for her to take a seat.

"Thanks, but I already poured some."

She plopped onto a stool, then gulped at her own coffee. It had gone cold. Before she could say anything, he took the cup from her and refilled it, then slid the squat carton of half-and-half toward her. How could he anticipate her needs like that? Loy felt a sudden stab of annoyance—or was it fear? She sloshed too much cream in her cup, then swished her spoon angrily against the stoneware edges. "So what did you want to talk about?" she asked in tones to match the click of the spoon.

"Breakfast first, remember?" He opened the refrigerator and inspected the contents. "What would you like? Eggs, pancakes, French toast?"

"Why don't you make yourself at home?" she invited with a heavy dash of cynicism.

"Thanks. Don't mind if I do," he returned easily, pulling out a handful of eggs and knocking the door shut with his elbow. "Where do you hide your pans?"

Loudly emitting a disgruntled sigh, she got up to help him. Together they soon had eggs, bacon, and toast heaped on plates and amid the tantalizing aromas Loy's irritation faded like so much steam. She couldn't hold on to her hostility and she didn't question how little she tried. They settled Jeeves in the garage with his own breakfast laced with bits of bacon and they sat at opposite sides of the dining table. Lavishly spreading butter on her toast, Loy admitted to herself she was glad he'd come. Being around him made her feel alive, special. She took an enormous bite out of the slice and smiled around the edges at him.

"When do you want to get married?" he asked, sounding precisely as if he were inquiring how the eggs tasted.

She gasped in astonishment. Toast stuck in her throat. She choked, coughing and spitting while blood rushed into her face. Her hair spilled free of its skewer to tumble down her back. Derett was up instantly and within seconds he'd handed her a glass of water. She swallowed eagerly, coughing a little between gulps and dribbling water down her bodice, until finally the toast was dislodged in a final hoarse rasp. When she could, Loy glared at Derett accusingly, but his twitching lips told her how ridiculous she must appear.

Stan's proposal had been, like the man himself, an oration filled with false charm. Keith's had been stolid, but endearing. This—this had been calculated, designed to make her feel vulnerable. And he hadn't even asked her *if* she'd marry him! It had been *when!* The arrogance of the man astounded her. She held herself rigidly and pronounced through stiff lips, "I hope you enjoyed your little joke. Shall we finish breakfast?"

He resumed his seat, spread his napkin back on his lap, and eyed her steadily. "It's not a joke, Loy."

She had known that. But knowing it and hearing him say it were two different things. She bent her head over her plate and picked up her fork. "It has to be," she said shakily. "I—you—we've only just met."

"So? I'm not talking about time. I'm talking about feelings." He steadily examined the two plates, the coffee swirling in the two cups. Then he raised his eyes to hers. They smoldered with determination and something else Loy had no wish to see. "Tell me you don't feel that being

101

together like this is *right*. Tell me you don't feel the certain perfection of it."

Loy pulled her eyes from his. She couldn't think clearly beneath the force of his heated gaze. Whatever her body desired, the last thing in the world Loy wanted was another marriage to fail at. The fork slid from her fingers to hit the plate with a resounding ping. Staring down at her clenched fists, she fortified herself with a deep breath. "It's out of the question."

"Why?" he shot back swiftly.

Dropping her napkin over her unfinished meal, she shoved the chair back and stood. "Because it is. I don't love you, for one thing. I don't intend to ever remarry, for another."

He followed her into the kitchen carrying his plate and looking for all the world as though discussing rejections of marriage were an everyday occurrence.

"Love can come," he stated firmly. As she started to deny this, knowing from past experience how untrue it was, he cut her off. "For us, it will come, Loy. I know how I feel. I know you feel the same. You just don't want to admit it."

"Not conceited, are you?" she muttered. She hit the faucet forcefully and rinsed the plates without looking at him.

"It's not conceit. It's just knowing that we belong together. We do belong together, Loy." When she didn't respond to this, he leaned casually against the refrigerator and watched her work. "As for the other . . . why not? What went so wrong in your marriage? If you like your ex so much—"

"Please quit calling him that!" She sucked in her lower lip to halt a further outburst. After she'd positioned the dishes in the dishwasher and shut the door with a slam that rattled the glasses within, she faced him defiantly. "How can you claim to know me? You don't know anything about me."

"So help me to change that. Open up to me. Let me know you."

Rain scurried against the windows, drumming in erratic counterpoint to her unsteady heartbeat. Loy felt locked into an eerie world, alone with the one man she most desired, most feared. She nervously swiped a dishrag over the counters, the stovetop, anything in sight. "What makes you think you . . . love . . . me? How can you know, just like that?" She snapped her fingers in the air for emphasis.

"I'm not an infatuated boy. I'm thirty-five years old and I've been around enough to know what I feel. I know I love you. I know I want you. I shake with wanting you."

The quiet vehemence of his words robbed her of speech, of breath, even of several heartbeats. He hadn't touched her, not with so much as a fingertip, yet she felt as if she'd been thoroughly manhandled. As if commanded by a caress, her breasts swelled against the confines of her blouse, the nipples extended tautly. Desire stirred, moist and tingly. The storm no longer raged outside; it raged within her. Her nerves bolted with the electricity of lightning. Her blood thundered with an aching she couldn't deny. She bent her head and her freed hair veiled her lovely face in a wild cascade.

He reached for her then. Knowing she should avoid him at all costs, she swayed into his arms. A certain feeling of inevitability took hold of Loy. This was a scene scripted by fate and the actors must play out their roles up to the final parting.

With an out-of-body feeling, Loy noted that his embrace was warm, that his arms were indeed trembling, that his breath misted her temple. Her palm pressed against the thin cotton of his shirt, against the driving beat of his heart. She arched her neck, tipping her head back, awaiting the heat of his lips to melt into hers. His warm breath caressed her. After a second or two she lifted her lids. Then she blinked.

A rueful smile tugged at his lips; a regretful gleam shone in his half-lidded eyes as he shook his head. "You're not ready for me, sweetheart. Not yet."

Not ready? Her mind shrieked with disbelief. What did he mean, not ready? She was dripping with readiness, aching with it!

Still wearing a half-mournful, half-amused expression, Derett put his hands on her shoulders and set her away from him. "First, we talk. Later, we'll love."

"Isn't that a little prosaic? Don't you believe in spontaneity? Or have you just been toying with me—again?" she snipped. Her ego was more than a little bruised. Could he always turn off his passions just like that? Some burning love he felt!

"A minute ago you were chiding me for my indulgence in spontaneity," he reminded her with a tap of his finger on her freckled nose. "We need to get things straight between us, Loy, before we get physical."

"If you were a woman, you'd be called a tease, do you know that?" Her voice shook with frustrated fury.

"I haven't been toying with you. Not now, not before. I've just been trying to make you realize what it is you want, what we both want." He clasped her by the shoulders, turned her around, and gently shoved her. "Now get yourself settled in the living room and I'll join you there shortly."

"Where are you going?" she demanded.

He shrugged, then displayed his dimples in a disarming, self-effacing smile. "I'm only human, sweet. I do feel physical enough to know that if we're going to talk, I've got to take a break from your body language."

She slid into the comfort of her chair, tucking her feet beneath her and wrapping her arms around herself. She should have her head examined, letting him dictate to her like this. After letting two men order her about—the one with cool contempt, the other with killing kindness—she'd vowed never, never, never to be ruled by another

104

man. Yet here she was, waiting for Derett at his direction. What was she, a woman or a mouse?

Loy avoided the larger, more frightening questions of what she felt, what she wanted, what she intended to do to keep Derett from propelling her into yet another disastrous marriage.

He came in quietly, his stockinged feet making no sound on the carpet. He held out a tall glass filled with orange juice over ice cubes. She ignored it, trying to look stern as she focused upon him. "You're crazy, you know that?"

"You're driving me crazy," he corrected her softly. He waved the glass under her nose and Loy gave in. She took it and sipped, then raised her eyes to his in silent inquiry.

"I added a little dash of gin," he explained. "You didn't have tomato juice for Bloody Marys and I figured we could use a little fortification. Jeeves, by the way, is flopped out in the garage, looking as if he never intends to move again."

"Ummm. I know. It's his favorite way to while away the day. When he isn't knocking me down or chasing leaves or informing the mailman he isn't wanted here, that is."

The jest was offered half-heartedly, but it served to lighten the oppressive fear closing in on Loy. She rotated her glass, listening to the ice jump against the sides and watching Derett sprawl nonchalantly over the couch. His long legs extended outward, crossed at the ankles as he dug his heels into the carpeting. He raised his glass in a wordless toast, then sipped.

"So what have you got against marrying me?"

"No softening chit-chat before you aim for the jugular?" she asked tartly, then glanced away from the heat in his eyes. Her tongue seemed stuck to her mouth, too heavy to move. Within the strained silence she noticed that the thunder had died away, though rain still pelted the house. She forced her tongue to work: "I'm no good at it. At marriage."

"One mistake doesn't mean," he began, only to stop at the emphatic shake of her head.

"Keith was mistake number two. So, you see, I really do know what I'm talking about. I'm a two-time loser, a flop, a fizzle, a washout in the marriage stakes." Her voice held equal parts of anger, fear, and self-reproach, and underscoring it all was lingering pain. She chanced a quick look at Derett. He sat silently contemplating his toes. A laugh so brittle, it crackled between them, escaped her.

His head came up and her laughter died at the expression on his face. Her heart hung suspended as he slowly set aside his glass and came to his feet. "You just married the wrong men. I'm the right one."

It was the calm assurance of his statement that slapped at her. She felt again the gut-wrenching agony of the uncertainty she'd suffered so often before. "Haven't you ever been unsure? Haven't you ever known what it is to doubt yourself?" she asked him irritably.

A slow smile touched his mouth. "What I don't doubt, my sweet Loy, is that you're going to marry me."

She plunked her own glass down with a furious whack and jumped angrily to her feet. "Don't you ever listen? Don't you understand? I don't *want* to get married!"

"What do you want?" he asked quietly.

Loy didn't even hesitate. She felt as if she'd spent a lifetime burning for Derett. She floated wordlessly into his arms. Pressing her body into the solid musculature of his, she murmured breathlessly, "This."

It was a complete offering. Loy curved pliantly into Derett. Tilting her head back, she tendered to him her mouth, her throat, each curve of her body. Her hair tangled over his hands; her heart met the frantic beat of his. Her breath mingled with his in the aching seconds before their lips melted together. Their tongues entwined and Loy shook with the hot pleasure of it.

Lips clinging to lips, they slid together to the floor. Derett traced the delicate structure of her face with his fingertips, his touch fervent yet silken. She mirrored the gesture, sculpting his features with a skimming of her fingers. He broke from her hold to push with feverish impatience at the scooped neck of her blouse. When he realized she wore no bra he softly moaned and suddenly slowed. With great deliberation he pulled her blouse from the waist of her slacks and gradually raised it over her head.

She wanted to shout at him to hurry, but when he at last exposed her breasts she had no breath with which to speak. She thought her heart would quit working altogether as he gently teased, playing with the fullness of each breast, circling the dark aureoles, then finally bending his head to nibble at the stiff buttons in turn.

Softly moaning, Loy dug her fingers into the muscles of his shoulders, his chest, his stomach, his hips. He felt solid and strong and *oh, dear lord,* deliciously responsive to her briefest caress. At the flick of her tongue in his ear he shuddered. At the graze of her fingers across his nape he groaned. When she ran one fingertip lightly down the metal of his zipper, he lifted his head to scorch her with the burning hunger of his gaze.

As one, they broke apart to fling free of their restrictive clothing. They paused, staring in reverent silence. She had thought him handsome when dressed. Standing before her naked, Derett was glorious—a tanned, tapered male animal whose muscles glistened in the faint shafts of the lamplight. The finest dusting of hair feathered his solid chest, forming a thin line that ran down his flat stomach. She gazed in awe at the sheer beauty of him. Then he reached for her.

They came together, flesh to flesh.

It was the thousandth time and it was the first time. Loy's knowledge of men, of sex, had not prepared her for the consuming need to meld her body with Derett's. Never had she wanted anything, anyone, so badly. Never had she needed as she needed now. He answered her need with the pulsing surge of his own.

And nothing had prepared her for the dizzying excitement as he crashed into her, filling her, making her his. She splayed her legs wider, wanting more of him, wanting all of him. Her fingers curled into the rippling muscles of his buttocks as they rose and fell in the fierce rhythm of possession. Loy gripped tightly and only later did she wonder at the irony of it, of holding on to him as she gave her soul away.

For now, she could not question the beauty, the rightness of it. For now, she could only delight in the spiraling passions bursting in her. The darting pleasures of his tongue over her lips, her jaw, her throat. The splintering sensations of his palms cupping her breasts. The throbbing fulfillment as she moved with him. Loy reveled in them all.

When he stiffened she tensed with him, flooded with an unbearable joy that drowned her senses. Gradually she realized he was gently stroking the hair from her brow. She opened her eyes and bathed in the love glinting in his.

"What's your home remedy for rug burns, Nightingale?" he queried, continuing to caress her temples.

"What?" She expected words of love, not talk of rugs.

"I have rug burns on my knees," he explained with hushed laughter. He rained kisses on her brows, her eyelids, her high cheekbones. "But don't think I'm complaining, sweetheart. It was more than worth it."

She looked down at his reddened knees and giggled. "No doubt my bottom is redder than your knees."

"I only ask—no, beg—to be the one to apply the remedy," he moaned against the fullness of her mouth.

Laughing, she shifted tantalizingly beneath him. She saw the instant glitter within his eyes and heard her laughter fade away. "I—I guess we should be getting up."

In answer, he bent his head to press his lips into the long arch of her neck. While he nibbled, his hands swirled playfully over the soft sides of her breasts.

"Derett—"

He skated kisses over her collarbone, then lower still, and slid his hands over the hollow beneath her ribs, around the slimness of her waist.

"Derett—"

He teased the line of her hips, deftly circling down to the curling mound between her thighs.

"Don't you think . . . we've had enough?" she finally managed to ask shakily.

He raised himself above her and brushed his tongue over the impassioned plumpness of her mouth. "I'll never get enough of you. Feel me. Feel how much I still want you."

Her hands obeyed his command, running down the lean sinews of his back and over the hard curves of his buttocks. He lay on his side and when she slid her hand down over his hip, he tensed, then released his breath in a low groan. He did want her again. He was ready for her.

But this time they prolonged the taking. This time they touched and explored and discovered. With exquisite sensitivity Derett restrained himself, seeking to satisfy her and giving Loy a depth of pleasure she'd never before known. When he nipped lightly at her earlobe, when he danced his fingers over her breasts, when he burrowed his lips into the hollow of her collarbone, she shuddered with a shattering rapture.

In turn, Loy let her hands drift over the tawny splendor of his skin, pausing here or there to tickle and tease and delight in his responses. With tiny nips that ranged from frisky to fierce, she tasted the tang of sweat glossing his skin. When she grazed her fingertips over the flat plane of his stomach, just below his navel, Derett inhaled so sharply she feared for an instant she'd somehow hurt him.

Unable to hold himself in check any longer, Derett took command. And still he possessed her slowly, gently. His unhurried cadence was a rich, warm, full display of his love. Loy accepted what he gave. She muffled the warnings sounding in her head and took the gift of his love. But she withheld giving the same commitment in return.

He stopped, full and hard within her, and waited until she opened her eyes. As she looked at him questioningly, his lips curled triumphantly. "Tell me . . . this isn't . . . right," he whispered hoarsely.

She shook her head from side to side, fanning her flaxen hair over the carpet. She couldn't say that. It was right, it was. But she couldn't say that either. His smile softened and she touched her fingers to the sweetness of it. "Don't talk . . . just love me."

"I do love you," he rasped.

She wiggled her hips to entice him to movement. She felt the soft warmth of his lips against her temple. Her mouth pressed against his jaw, savoring the hard bone beneath the firm skin. He turned his head quickly, swooping over her lips in a savage kiss.

"And you, Loy McDaniel," he groaned at the edge of her mouth, "you love me."

Before she could deny this, he thrust forward, slowly at first, then with gathering tempo. She forgot everything but her longing for release and worked to flow with him. When his need was at its height, he called out her name in a voice husked with love. And Loy, beyond knowing what she did, returned the call, crying, "Derett, Derett, Derett," until the pleasure swept over her totally.

It was a cry that was to return to her again and again in the weeks to come.

CHAPTER EIGHT

Loy felt wonderfully, wickedly wanton.

She lay curled in Derett's arms amid a variegation of discarded clothing, sheltered from the world beyond by the continuing storm. Though her eyes were closed she could still see the beauty of their bodies twined together, bathed in the muted glow of the single burning lamp. She could see the powerful flexure of muscles beneath his tawny skin, could feel the slick sheen of sweat oiling his virile physique as he worked to make her his. She saw and felt and knew again the throbbing pleasure of it.

Had she ever before known such an overpowering need? Or so deliciously given in to it? Her mouth slid languidly up in a satisfied smile.

"Ummm, that looks good enough to kiss," murmured Derett as he suited action to word.

He kissed her playfully, tugging on her lips, then nibbling lightly at the edges. His lips lingered above hers, tenderly teasing, before he drew back slightly. He slid his hand down to the curve of her hip, up to the underside of her breasts and back down again. His touch was exquisitely delicate and Loy quivered beneath his fingertips.

"You know, my family's always accusing me of lacking ambition, but I now have a definite goal which ought to keep me occupied, oh, a mere lifetime or so."

Her lashes lifted slowly. When she peered at him through the fringe, her heart flipped. The light in his eyes as he gazed at her gleamed darkly of desire, brightly of love. It took her breath away to see him looking at her that way and Loy could barely whisper, "What?"

He bent his head closer to drop a kiss on the bridge of her nose. "It's my lifetime ambition, my dearest love, to kiss each freckle you possess."

She laughed unsteadily. "But I have freckles on my—"

"So I've discovered." He raised his brows, tilting the spliced one. "Why do you think I'm so determined?"

"Oh, Derett, what am I to do with you?"

"You asking for suggestions?"

Her arms tightened about him. Feelings she couldn't begin to understand washed over her. Thrill in being with him. Joy in being a woman for him. Fear that he could make her feel this way. He nuzzled her breasts and goose bumps rose where the sandy softness of his hair caressed her skin. She tried to think, to distract herself from her confusing, frightening whirl of emotions.

"I—you—this—" she stuttered.

He lifted his head and smiled and her heart thumped against the lingering heat of his last kiss. "Yes?"

"This has been . . . like . . . spontaneous combustion. We just . . . ignited. . . ."

His smile became both tender and triumphant. "I knew. The moment I saw you, love, I knew it would be like this for us. I saw you and starting shaking. Half the photos I took that day came out fuzzy."

"I started shaking, too—I was so furious, I couldn't stop trembling," she confessed on an intimate giggle.

"You were trembling now too . . . with much better reason."

The husk of his words, the darkening of his gaze, warned Loy that his desire still simmered, ready to boil over at her merest breath. She thought if they made love again she would indeed combust; she would disappear in a bursting flame of raw passion. Seeking to lighten the mood, she flicked her eyes over him and mused, "I didn't see your birthmark, Derett. Where is it?"

112

"Ah, the birthmark."

"Yes, the infamous birthmark." She met his chuckle with a mock frown.

"Maybe you should look again," he suggested provocatively.

"Just tell me where it is."

"We-e-e-ell . . ." He dragged the word out on a warm expulsion of breath into her ear. He grinned, denting his dimples at her. "I have to confess, ma'am. I lied about the birthmark."

"Oh! You—" She aimed a slap at his rear, but he swiftly slid beyond her reach. He grimaced as he moved and Loy lowered her hand. "What's wrong?"

"My knees. I wasn't lying about the rug burns." He sat up and pulled his knees forward. Loy could see the reddened abrasions on the kneecaps, but somehow she couldn't summon up any sympathy. Nor could she stifle her bubble of laughter. He shot her a sour look, then grinned despite himself. "Not very romantic, is it? We'll just have to restrict ourselves to the bedroom when we're married."

The word, spoken so naturally, so confidently, totally doused the embers of her passion. Jerking upright like a puppet yanked on a string, Loy gaped at him in horror. "We're not getting married!" she exclaimed baldly.

It was Derett's turn to gape. Then his mouth slowly curved into a coaxing smile, and his eyes shone with a composed resolution which maddened her. "Of course we are, sweetheart. You can't think I'm simply lusting after your body—though I admit, if I wanted to lust after a body, it would definitely be yours." She didn't acknowledge the joke, and after a strained pause he said with soft seriousness, "I love you. I want to be with you."

Loy suddenly understood her earlier fear. He didn't know, he couldn't understand how marriage could suffocate the soul. He didn't understand that love didn't last. He didn't know how two people no longer in love could tear at each other bit by bit. He didn't know the pain and hurt of breaking up. She knew. She knew that love for her wasn't a lasting thing. She knew the trauma of ending a marriage. She knew she couldn't go through it again.

Her eyes flew about the room and the beauty she'd seen in the piles of clothes strewn over the floor now appeared tarnished, tawdry. She felt ridiculous sitting there naked. Abruptly she grabbed a handful of clothes and held them before her, shielding her body from his eyes. The action was a mistake, imbuing what they'd done with a cheapness that hadn't been there at all. Loy saw her mistake when she cast a sidelong glance at Derett. His lips thinned to a single line and his eyes smoldered with a searing anger. She made a movement to stand, but he reacted swiftly, clasping her wrist and yanking her down in one motion. When she thumped back onto the floor, he reached for the clothes she still held before her chest.

"Don't!" she cried.

He wrenched the blouse and slacks from her hands and tossed them aside. "Don't. Don't hide yourself from me, Loy. This isn't dirty or shameful. It's beautiful. You're beautiful."

She scrambled for the clothes and he pushed her roughly away from them. She accepted defeat then. Not looking at him, head bent as if to hide behind the crinkling disarray of her long hair, she mumbled, "Please. I can't talk like this."

The heat of his steady gaze singed her. In the seconds that she struggled for a breath, Loy wondered why it had all gone so wrong. It had been so right. Suddenly her clothes dropped in her lap. She looked nervously at him.

His face was blank. His voice was toneless. "I'm sorry. Get dressed and we'll talk."

She didn't wait for him to change his mind. Her dash to the bathroom would have qualified her for the world sprinting record. Once there, she thrust herself into her clothes, then dampened a washrag with cold water and held it to her burning face. When she lowered the cloth she realized how foolishly she'd been acting. Derett hadn't misled her. He'd told her before that he wanted to marry her. After such wild, passionate lovemaking, it was only natural he'd assume her feelings were the same. She simply hadn't made it clear to him that they could have a relationship without marriage. She tried on a smile. It was crooked. With a shrug she went back to the living room.

He wasn't there. She found him in the kitchen, sitting on a stool with his elbows propped on the counter and his interlaced fingers pressed against his thinned lips. He didn't look at her when she came in, but inquired over his knuckles, "Do you feel cleaner? Safer? Both?"

"I'm sorry, Derett. I didn't mean to ruin things. You . . . scared me and I . . . I just overreacted."

For two terrible heartbeats she thought he wasn't going to accept her apology. Then his hands came down and he swiveled around to face her. She saw a mixture of emotions play over his face—anger, puzzlement, resignation, and most of all, love. Without even thinking, she responded to the love. She met his darkened gaze without flinching, then crossed to him and pressed her palms against the planes of his cheeks. She kissed him softly. "Forgive me," she whispered against his mouth.

His arms came around her. "I already have."

They held on to each other a moment more, then broke apart to examine the other's face somewhat warily. Loy saw the firm set of Derett's jaw, the implacable determination in his green eyes, and knew she was going to have trouble convincing him to forget the idea of marriage. He wasn't the type of man to concede easily and she already knew he had the strength of will to rival a steel mill. But she also saw his love-tousled hair, the full touch of passion on his lower lip, and knew she had at least one card with which to trump him.

"Now," she said briskly as she pulled away from his hold, "tell me why you're so set on marriage. I thought men these days still wanted to remain footloose and fancy free."

"Tell me why you're so set against it. I thought women these days still wanted the security of home and husband."

"I asked you first. Would you like some lunch?" He nodded and got up to help her dig out sandwich makings. Lining up mayonnaise and mustard jars, she glanced sidelong at him, "Why can't we just have each other and enjoy it?"

Derett handed her a loaf of whole wheat bread and a pack of luncheon meat. "I want to settle down, Loy. I've been traveling around the world for over a decade now and I'm tired of being footloose and fancy free. Believe me, it's not what it's cracked up to be. I'm ready to set down roots, make a home. I'm ready for a wife, a family. I want kids." He paused. "You want kids?"

She slapped some mayonnaise on the bread with vigor. "I don't know. Hadn't thought about it." She couldn't meet his eyes, but knew he was watching her, probing. "You want lettuce?"

"I want you."

The lettuce leaf dangled in mid-air for just a fraction of time, then landed on the bread. "I want you too, Derett."

"Then why—"

"I don't want any longterm commitments." She swung toward him, pleading for understanding with her troubled gaze. "Let's just enjoy what we've got, for as long as it lasts."

"I want it—us—to last a lifetime. That means making a commitment."

"Marriage isn't a guarantee, Derett!" Loy clapped the knife to the counter with a reverberating clatter. "I have good reason—*two* very good reasons—to know that it isn't. Really, you're old enough to know that nothing lasts a lifetime. Nothing. Certainly not love."

She pitched the sandwich onto a plate and shoved it

toward him. He took it, then set it aside. "I don't know about that. I've never been in love before."

Loy halted in the process of picking up her own plate. "Never?" she said in shrill disbelief.

"Never. At least not the kind where I felt this consuming need to be with someone all the time."

She continued to stare at him, her mouth slightly agape. She didn't know how to act, how to react to him. Something in his stance changed, relaxed. He picked up his plate and walked into the dining room. Loy followed him.

He began speaking as she sat to his right. "I've been the despair of my family. They're very old-fashioned. My brother Wes once told me if I weren't getting married, I should go into the priesthood, as if bachelorhood for any other purpose were a sin."

"You're Catholic?"

"Lapsed. But, yes, still Catholic. Does that bother you?"

"Of course not. Why should it?"

"Because our children would be raised in the church."

She set her sandwich down and bent her head. When she felt she could speak without stammering, she lifted her eyes to his. "Please, don't. I can't accept what you're saying. I can't take being rushed like this. It happened to me twice before and I can't allow myself to make a third mistake."

"Is that how you think of me—as a mistake?"

She shivered at the sting in his tone. She shook her head. "No, not you. Marriage. Marriage is a mistake for me. I told you, I'm no good at it."

He ate for a time in silence. She tried to eat, but gave up. Everything was sticking in her throat. When he was done, she stood up, but he motioned for her to sit. She sat.

"Do you love me?" he asked in a voice void of emotion.

"I . . ." She bit her lip, then whispered, "I don't know."

"I see."

His chair went back with a crash and he was standing

117

stiffly before her. Loy gazed up at him in shock. He didn't see, he didn't see at all. His face was set and cold, his eyes were dark with furious pain. She opened her mouth, but nothing came out. Nothing could get past the lump in her throat.

"I see that for you this was just a sexual interlude," he bit out. "Tell me, do you often sleep with men you don't love? Is this why your marriages failed?"

The questions were harsh, meant to hurt. They did hurt. They hurt like hell. But instead of denying, explaining, reasoning with him, Loy bent her head over the hands twisting together in her lap and said nothing at all. She felt Derett's anger wordlessly slap at her. Still she could say nothing, do nothing.

A distant wail broke the strained silence. For once incredible second Loy thought perhaps she'd keened in bitter lamentation. Jeeves again howled for freedom, Derett pivoted, and she realized she'd lost her chance to keep him from leaving. She sat down, numb. Two large tears glistened down her cheeks, followed by a steady, silent track.

Why should she cry? She should be glad it was ended before it began. It could only be worse as time went on. The longer it went on, the greater her failure, the deeper the wound. She'd been saved all the bitter anguish of another divorce. She should be happy. Perhaps they were tears of joy.

Somewhere at the back of her mind, she heard the opening of a door, a happy bark, footsteps returning. Jeeves bounded toward her, then stopped abruptly and sat on his haunches, whimpering. He couldn't stand it when she cried. It was as if her pain were his pain. Loy swallowed, trying for his sake to stop the flow.

"Stop crying," snapped Derett.

Perversely, fresh tears spilled over her lashes, clumping them together and joining the rivulets sliding down to her chin. A half-growl, half-groan sounded from Derett and then he was beside her, pulling her up from the chair, circling her with his arms, stroking her hair.

"I'm sorry, don't cry, I didn't mean it," he rasped into her ear. "I know you're not that kind of woman."

She sniffled loudly and burrowed her head farther into the comforting warmth of his shoulder. "I know," she mumbled.

"I just wanted to hurt you."

"I know."

His hold constricted her. His lips pressed against her hair. "I wasn't being fair. I've waited so long for love, I guess I just expected you to feel what I feel. And after . . . it felt so *right* . . ."

"I know."

He took a step back and lifted her head. Cupping her chin with his palms, he rubbed his thumbs gently over her wet cheeks. "You know so much, how come you don't know you love me?"

She shook her head wordlessly, unable to speak. What could she say that wouldn't magnify the piercing pain she felt, he felt? How could she explain that love wasn't something she succeeded at? She shuddered and another tear slid slowly down her stained face.

He covered her trembling lips with a kiss of infinite tenderness. He pulled back, still cradling her head, and said slowly, "You do love me, darling. And together we can make our love last."

A nose nuzzled Loy's knee. She looked down to see Jeeves staring at her with soulful brown eyes. Grateful for the excuse to break away from the shattering emotions that threatened to overwhelm her, Loy knelt and hugged him. "It's okay, boy. I'm okay." She fluffed his floppy ears and looked past the top of his head to Derett. "I'm okay," she repeated firmly.

Derett righted his overturned chair. Jeeves licked her hand, then wandered off in search of his water bowl. Loy stood. She collected the plates from the table, not looking at Derett as he trailed behind her into the kitchen. He leaned against the counter while she stacked the dishes in the sink. She could feel the potency of his gaze upon her.

"We laugh at the same things," he quietly remarked.

She rinsed one plate and positioned it in the dishwasher. She picked up the second, then set it down and turned off the water. "Don't press me, Derett," she said without turning.

"We could share so much more than just laughter. We could share a lifetime."

A vague reflection of him wavered on the rain-splattered windowpane above the sink. Loy lowered her gaze to the stainless steel appliance. "I warned you before—I'm incapable of giving you what you want. If you insist on demanding what I can't give you, we'll have to put a stop to this. Now. Before it gets any worse."

She heard the scraping of his blue jeans as he shifted. She heard his footstep fall behind her.

"What do you want then, Loy? A summer affair?" His voice held the harsh ring of a sneer.

She whirled. "Don't! Don't put an ugly label on something that could be beautiful."

"Beautiful and brief."

Hopelessness washed over her. She shrugged. "How could you think we could make a marriage work? It's only taken us a couple of hours to ruin our relationship."

He stared down at her, his eyes hidden by the length of his lashes. "What relationship?"

Loy wasn't deceived by the mildness of his question. Tension radiated from him like atomic heat. She cleared her throat and said lamely, "This one."

From the corner came a growl that was almost a plea. Derett glanced over his shoulder. Jeeves sat on his haunches, his wide, liquid eyes swerving from one to the other.

"He hates arguments of any kind," explained Loy lifelessly.

Derett looked back at her. To her surprise a smile spread slowly over his mouth. "I wouldn't upset Jeeves for the world. Or you." He paused. "At least you do admit we have some sort of relationship. That's a start."

"It's all we can ever have," she said, turning back to the sink. "You have to accept things as they are, Derett. I just couldn't take being torn apart by another marriage."

He moved behind her, molding his solid form against the soft curves of her back. His arms encircled her and his lips brushed the top of her hair. "I won't tear you apart, darling, I swear it." She stiffened within his embrace. He let her go, but did not step from behind her. "I'll accept the status quo, but you have to promise me something in return."

Gripping the edge of the sink until her knuckles whitened, she asked, "What?"

"That you'll stop thinking of me as a threat to you. Think of me as who I am, Loy, not anything or anyone else. Don't compare me to your ex-husbands—"

"I haven't—"

"Haven't you? Haven't you been afraid to let yourself love me because of what happened with them? It's not what I've done or wanted that's become the axis of our relationship, but what they did. I'm not like them and I'm damn well going to prove that to you."

She wanted to be honest with him, to explain that it wasn't Stan or Keith that was the problem. They both had successful second marriages. *She* was the problem. She was the one who hadn't pleased Stan enough, the one who hadn't loved Keith enough. She was the one who couldn't make a marriage work.

But Loy thought of the surging brightness of loving Derett and kept silent. To share the love and the laughter with him—if even only briefly—was a need so overwhelming, she stifled the impulse to make him understand. Instead, she swung to face him. "Let's not analyze or label or think! Let's just experience what we've got while we've got it!"

He replied by taking her into his arms. As his hands tangled into the disarray of her hair, her mouth eagerly accepted the fierce mastery of his. She arched toward him, raising her arms to wreath his neck. His breath met hers in a soft moan.

A low whine escalated to a series of sharp yips. Derett reluctantly lifted his head. "What the hell—"

"Worse than arguments, Jeeves can't stand lovemaking," said Loy on a breathy laugh. "It makes him feel left out."

"He's just—" He broke off to kiss her lightly on the brow. Jeeves whimpered at the painful sight.

"Going to have to accept—" He rained brief kisses over both eyelids and the tip of her nose. The dog barked mournfully.

"Having his sensibilities offended." Derett lowered his lips to hers, playfulness melding with passion. Jeeves bounded forward in a single leap to bump against their legs. They tried to ignore him, but he rose on his hind legs and leaned insistently into them. The trio toppled to the linoleum in a heap of laughter and yelps.

"Some chaperon you have here," said Derett when he finally unraveled himself from the jumble.

She peered up at him from beneath her lashes. She accepted the hand he held out and as he hauled her to her feet, she expanded, "An improved form of chastity belt."

Jeeves lumbered after them, ready to play more games. Derett shook his fist at the dog and threatened to call Animal Control. "And as for you, lady," he added, closing in on the laughing Loy, "if you don't stop that howling, they'll pick up the wrong animal."

"Watch it, Graham, or I'll blister more than just your knees," she warned with the heaviest scowl she could manufacture.

"Is that a promise?" he asked, once again effectively impeding the flow of Loy's breath.

The steady drizzling continued, but failed to dampen their spirits. Derett suggested they go meander through Oak Park Mall and Loy agreed readily. They whiled away the afternoon strolling through the gigantic mall, wandering in and out of shops and spending thousands of imaginary dollars on everything from sneakers to satin sheets.

At one point Loy discovered that Derett had been right. They did indeed laugh at the same things. Sitting in one of the mall's rest areas, shaded by a leafy tree and lulled by the gurgling murmur of a running fountain, they watched a woman with an armload of shopping bags sink wearily to the bench across from them. As one bag slipped from her hands, she shifted the others, struggling to retrieve it. Just as she sat upright with the bag triumphantly in her hand, another slid to the floor. This happened again and again, until the poor woman was scarlet from her exertion. Why she didn't set her packages on the bench, Loy couldn't understand and it was all she could do not to laugh outright. It was as she was smiling in amusement that Loy noticed Derett was smiling in exactly the same way. They exchanged their smiles and moved on, but she didn't forget the moment.

They made one purchase. Derett bought a new polarizing filter, telling Loy that he'd like to try exaggerating the contrast between the natural blue of the sky and the color of the balloon the next time they were out flying. It reminded her that their time together was limited, but she hid that from him by asking lightly why he had come to Kansas City in the first place.

"I was here last fall doing a bit for Jeff on the American Royal. I really liked it here—K.C. is such a mixture of metropolitan and downhome—and when I decided a needed a break, I came back. I leased my house for a year,

123

intending to laze around for six months before looking for assignments in the area."

He sent her a look that made her legs go weak. She riveted her gaze on the in-mall theaters they were passing and inhaled the warm aroma of buttered popcorn. She kept her eyes on the movie posters and asked lightly, "How do you find jobs?"

"You mean when I'm not finagling my way into a lady's affections?" he queried, chuckling. "I have an agent. Some assignments he tosses at me, some ideas I toss at him and let him find where to place them. Though my writing's improved over the years, I still rely mostly on my photography; it's what I do best."

Loy privately thought his real expertise lay in another direction altogether, but she didn't tell him this. His confidence in that area was already more than healthy enough. They walked on, sometimes talking, sometimes not, just enjoying being together. When they'd been in and out of nearly every store in the mall, they headed for the parking lot and home.

They walked in, greeted Jeeves, and hung up their raincoats side by side in the foyer closet. It seemed natural, as if they'd done such things a hundred times before. A small frown sketched Loy's brow as she went into the kitchen. She could hear Derett moving in the living room, heard the low hum of voices when he turned on the television. It was as if he belonged here.

She puttered about in the kitchen, stalling, then called Gary and the Perren brothers to tell them what they already knew, that there'd be no flight tonight. Roger told her that they'd finally gotten a "great set of wheels" and would be able to crew in the morning if she needed them. Groaning cheerfully, he agreed to meet at the usual time and place. Laughing at his lack of enthusiasm about the time, she told him she'd see him there and hung up. When she turned around she nearly jumped out of her skin. Derett was standing a mere foot away.

124

"God! You scared the life out of me!" she exclaimed, her hand on her thumping heart.

"Sorry."

He didn't sound sorry. In fact, he was scowling at her, his jaw pugnaciously set. Wondering what on earth had gotten under his skin, Loy offered a placating smile. "That's okay. I just didn't hear you."

"Who was that you just agreed to meet?"

She stared a moment, not comprehending. When she did, her ever-ready temper flared. "None of your business!"

But, as always, Derett didn't do what she expected him to. Instead of reacting with a greater show of anger, his own ill humor seemed to fade beneath the force of hers. He shook his head, looking rather like a disappointed parent facing a recalcitrant child. "When are you going to get it through that beautiful brain of yours that whatever you do *is* my business?"

"When you get it through that thick head of yours that I live my own life, not somebody else's!" she retorted. "How would you like it if I quizzed you about every phone call you made?"

"You wouldn't have to. I'd offer the information freely."

"You didn't give me a chance to tell you a thing before biting my head off just now." She frowned at him. "And why aren't you angry anymore? You looked mad as hell then."

He smiled. "I'm not angry because as soon as you yelled at me, I realized I was acting like an ass. And you're right. I wasn't giving you a chance to tell me anything." His dimples indented as his mouth quirked. "Forgive me?"

She tried to frown harder, but knew she couldn't resist returning his smile. "Oh, you know I do," she huffed. Then, giving into the inevitable, she smiled and reluctantly admitted, "It was Roger I agreed to meet—for our flight tomorrow morning. He and Danny bought a van. If it's

125

anything like the bug, it's probably held together by the rust."

"So tonight's definitely off?"

"Yes. I'm just about to call my charter and let them know the bad news. I'll reschedule them and then come back to get started on supper. Would you like to stay for supper?"

She was walking toward her office as she spoke. His reply halted her in mid-step.

"I'd like to stay for the night."

Several emotions warred within her. Elation emerged victorious. She blew him a saucy kiss and skipped down the hall. Heartbreak, she decided, would have to wait for another day. For now, she had the night—and Derett.

CHAPTER NINE

"So, have you set a date?"

Lisle Craeger was nothing if not tenacious. She fixed her clear blue eyes steadily on her younger sister and waited for an answer to her question.

Playing with the red plastic swizzle stick in her daiquiri, Loy sighed. She'd done her best to ignore the oblique hints all morning long, but obviously Lisle had now decided to be blunt. She glanced over the colorful flow of traffic surrounding the sidewalk café and finally settled her gaze on one of the many stone fountains to be found in the Plaza. Striving for a bright tone, she queried in reply, "You mean for the barbecue? Yes, I've—"

"I'm not talking barbecue and you know it," cut in Lisle firmly. She hooked her amber hair behind each ear and leaned back in her chair. "I'm talking about a wedding date. You know—dum-dum-da-dummmm."

The babble of voices, the clink of plates and glasses, the clipclop of horse-drawn carriages, and the drone of cars blended in a symphony around them. The noontime sun richocheted from mosaic-topped buildings to gaily striped umbrellas yawning over the round tables. Loy sipped at her drink, staring at the shadow of their umbrella's fringe. As little as she liked confrontations, she knew nothing less than plain speaking would suffice. She set down her glass and at last eyed Lisle directly.

"No, we haven't set a date and"—she held up her hand to halt an interruption—"we aren't going to. I know you

127

care, sis, and I'm touched that you do, but don't push, okay? We're happy with things as they are."

"I know you're happy. I've never seen you so happy. You've been sparkling like a tinseled Christmas tree for the past month. And if you don't know why, I'll tell you." Lisle reached over the tabletop to lay her fingers over Loy's. "You're in love."

A soft smile settled upon Loy. She turned her hand to clasp her sister's. "I know," she murmured.

"Well, then . . . ?"

"Well, then what? I'm in love—deliriously, wondrously, in love—I admit it. So let me enjoy it; don't spoil my happiness with useless arguments about marriage." She squeezed Lisle's hand, then released it to nervously adjust the tangerine combs holding her hair back above each ear.

Lisle fished the strawberry from the midst of her own drink and studied it with intense concentration before eating it in one bite. Wiping her fingers on her napkin, she remarked casually, "A blind man can see that Derett worships the ground you walk on."

"I know," said Loy again, her lips curving with that same, satisfied smile. She did know, she knew precisely how Derett felt because he'd taken every opportunity over the past weeks to let her know. They had shared love and laughter—and champagne.

That first glorious night had been the beginning of the enchantment. They talked and laughed companionably over a leisurely supper, then were swept away by the passion that had been roiling beneath the surface. Within the quilted folds of the comforter on Loy's brass bed, they had touched in a mutual surrender of the senses. Pleasure was given and received until they drifted together into sleep.

Something tickled her nose. Loy hadn't wanted to wake up from her delightful dreams. She wrinkled her nose, then waved a languorous hand to brush it away. Instead, the fizzing reached her lips. She opened her eyes to see

Derett dipping a fingertip in a glass of champagne. As she watched, he set the fingertip to her lips, then bent to flick the bubbles away with his tongue.

Even now, bathed in sticky sunshine amid the protean public, Loy could feel again the hot rush of desire that had wakened with her that night. With bubbles of champagne clinging to each kiss, they had come together in the shadows. She had known then that she loved Derett, loved him as she'd never loved another man. And that very depth frightened her more than anything else, for she was certain it meant her eventual heartbreak was going to be all the worse. But she'd thrust such fears away that night, crying his name instead of her love as she rose to meet him at the pinnacle of passion.

A finger snapped in front of her gaze and Loy blinked, startled. "Earth to Loy, are you there?" inquired Lisle, snapping her fingers a second time.

"I—yes, I'm here," she answered on a self-conscious laugh.

"I thought I'd have to send a spaceman after you."

"Sorry. I was just . . . daydreaming."

"From the gleam in your eyes, it isn't hard to guess about whom. As I was saying, you two are wild about each other. So why keep trying to fight it?"

"I'm not fighting anything," muttered Loy with a heavy sigh. "Look, we're happy. You should be glad there's no marriage to mess things up between us. Derett's satisfied, why can't you be?"

Lisle's sculpted brows rose and she eyed her sister sharply. "You mean he hasn't asked you to marry him?"

"Well . . ."

"There!" she exclaimed triumphantly. "You see? Marry him, Loy. If you don't, you'll regret it."

Loy impatiently plucked the plastic stick from her drink and bent it in two. "He did ask me, once. But only once and that was . . . before. I don't understand your persistence about this, Lisle. We don't need a certificate and a ring to be happy."

A noise somewhere between a sniff of disdain and a snort of disbelief met this pronouncement. "If ever there was a man wanting to be married, that man is yours. Every time we've seen him, he's gone crazy over Becky and Jason. He wants children, Loy, and the wife and mother to go with them. And he's just the type to insist on the certificate and ring to get them."

Shrugging away the nagging suspicion that her sister spoke the unadulterated truth, Loy downed the rest of her daiquiri and reached for her purse. She extracted a bill and some change, laying the money beside her empty glass. "Anyone would think I was an adolescent dealing with her first crush, to hear you dish out the advice. I think I can handle my own affairs."

Lisle stared at her for a long moment, then stood. "That's the operative word, isn't it?"

Nothing more was said as the sisters walked out of the courtyard café. They crossed the street and clipped along Brush Creek Boulevard without so much as glancing at each other. The kaleidoscope of people and traffic changed patterns unnoticed. Fountains and statues were passed unseen. Even the eye-catching displays in store windows failed to snare Loy's attention. Her mind was fully occupied.

She knew Lisle had meant well, and she even, in her heart, agreed with much of what her sister said. But she wasn't ready to contemplate another leap into the marital stakes. She'd already come out as a two-time loser; it upset her that Lisle didn't understand how scared she was.

A horn blared and Loy jumped back to the curb. There were no traffic signals or signs within the Plaza itself, and though the pedestrian supposedly had the right of way, it was a dubious right when faced with a ton of automobile barreling down the street. As Loy jerked to a halt, Lisle braced her back.

"Hey, there's no reason to get yourself flattened on my account," she said hurriedly. She gave Loy a quick hug before releasing her. "You okay?"

Loy pulled the strap of her purse back up on her shoulder and nodded. "Just shaken up a bit. I didn't even see that guy!"

Putting out a hand, Lisle said slowly, "Loy—I'm sorry. I don't mean to interfere. Still friends?"

"Still friends," she agreed with a lopsided smile. Checking the traffic both ways, they moved on and Loy queried, "Are you doing anything on the Fourth?"

"Nothing planned. Why?"

"I've talked about having a barbecue for weeks. It's about time I actually had one. What better time than the Fourth of July to hold a barbecue?"

"Sounds great. What time and what should I bring?"

"Oh, I don't know—fourish?" At Lisle's confirming nod, she paused to flash a grin. "There's no need, although I'd readily eat your infamous potato salad."

She cheerfully assented to provide the potato salad, and while they browsed through several of the Plaza's specialty shops they discussed preparations and plans for the "shindig" as Lisle termed it. They carefully avoided any return to the topic that had threatened to ruin their day. But on the way home their chatter faded away and thoughts of Derett Graham loomed within Lisle's compact station wagon. Loy stared unseeing out the passenger window and drifted back into daydreams.

Visions of Derett crowded everything else from her mind. Derett in the afternoon, kneeling in the backyard with sudsy water splattered from head to toe as he washed an unwilling Jeeves. She recalled her laughter as with a mighty shake that soaked Derett completely, Jeeves escaped. And, seconds later, her outraged shriek as he scooped her up and threw her into the plastic pool of swirling suds and dirty water. He muffled her shouts by tumbling in on top of her and kissing her into submission.

Later they'd showered and loved and whispered words that added yet another link in the chain binding Loy to him. The memory of it draped a wistful cloak over her. She didn't want to be bound to him in any way. She wanted their love to be free, unfettered. She focused her gaze on the car just ahead of them.

And she saw Derett in the mornings, leaning against the rim of the gondola, one hand on the burner and the other lazily stroking her thigh. He glanced down at her. His hand ceased to move, branding her skin where it lay. "Let's try it in here," he suggested, his voice husked with desire.

"Derett! We can't!" she protested, laughing. "We'd crash."

"But what a way to go, eh?" He quirked his brows and displayed his dimples, then reached for her. "Let's at least see how far we can get."

"Are you crazy?" she asked on a gasp as he slid his hands beneath her tank top. He lifted the mauve material and bent his mouth to her exposed breast. "You're crazy!" she rasped, then moaned.

"Ummm," he murmured in agreement.

The hum of his lips against her nipple shattered the flimsy wall of her resistance. Cradling his head with her palms, she pulled insistently until he lifted his lips to hers. They pressed together with wild abandonment. The basket rocked heavily, jolting them apart. As they swayed toward one another, Loy saw the clump of branches and managed to puff, "Trees!"

He reacted slowly, his arms still stretching for her, but then, realizing the danger, turned instead to the burner. Leaves rustled against the bottom of the wicker as they scraped the treetops. Loy leaned out over the basket and grabbed a handful of leaves. When they began to float upward, she stuffed them down his jeans and the madness had started all over again.

And most of all, Loy saw Derett at night. He stayed

132

with her three or four nights a week and they were the golden memories, the ones she would treasure for the rest of her life. She shivered as she envisioned his tawny skin gleaming in the silken night-shadows as he lay next to her. Her fingers tingled at the thought of the soft down of hair contrasting with the firm muscles beneath. The image of his long legs wrapped around hers flashed in her mind and her blood began to pound through her veins.

She sat upright, feeling wildly disoriented as she realized the car had stopped. They were parked in her driveway. Loy gazed at her house, then turned to look at Lisle.

"Welcome back."

Loy flushed. If she had been caught in the act, she doubted she could have felt any more embarrassed than she did beneath that knowing smile of Lisle's. "Uh, well, thanks for the ride and—and the shopping and all."

She opened the door, but Lisle held her a moment. "Loy, I promise I won't say another word about this, but—no, please listen! Don't keep Derett dangling too long. He's not the type to dance on a string, Loy, and if you don't give him all your love, you may lose him."

Not looking at Lisle, Loy slid out of the car and stood back to silently wave as the station wagon backed out onto the street. No matter what her sister believed, Loy was unalterably certain marriage would only ruin what she and Derett had together. Things had been so wonderful for them, she had no wish to risk spoiling it by shackling Derett to her. By the time Lisle's car was out of sight, Loy had convinced herself Derett didn't really want the risk either.

Contentment sheathed her like a custom-made suit. Loy snuggled deeper into Derett's arms and purred happily.

"You like this?" he asked, his breath stirring the tendrils of hair wisping over her ears.

"I love it," she answered on a sigh.

The evening had been extra special. After a week that

133

had seemed oddly strained between them—a fact Loy refused to attribute to her disturbing discussion with Lisle —tonight had returned to the glowing magic that had made her time with Derett so sublimely memorable. Tonight had been a celebration.

Derett had passed his oral and written exams and excelled during his check flight. He'd been duly licensed as a pilot for lighter-than-air craft. To celebrate, Loy arranged with a close friend to take out her charter for the night while they enjoyed a rare night on the town. They ate at one of the city's finest restaurants, the Alameda, where they sat at a window overlooking the Plaza. After a sumptuous and elegantly served meal, Loy was given a red rose as they left. Alone in the outside glass elevator that descended from the restaurant, she inhaled its perfume while Derett fingered the petals.

"Shall I pin it on for you?" he asked, eyeing her critically.

She wore a black crepe dress with a halter top and a full skirt that swished about her long legs whenever she moved. Her hair was pinned carefully atop her head, with selected curls falling artfully about her nape and high cheeks. Diamond teardrops ornamented her ears, glittering with each breath she took. Sparkles radiated from them as she shook her head. "No, I'll carry it."

Derett expelled a drawn-out sigh. "I had my hopes of putting it just . . . there," he said, sketching a fingertip over the swell of her left breast. Tiny goose bumps rose in the path he traced. Loy drew in a breath.

"Or maybe here," he mused, moving to the other side. She watched the gradual progress of his finger over the thin material and shivered.

"Or—" His finger dipped to the creamy skin glistening in the center V and Loy slapped his hand away.

"Be good!" she whispered furiously as the doors opened on a sharp ping. His soft chuckle followed her out of the elevator and through the knot of people waiting to get in.

134

He caught her elbow in his hand and bent his lips to her ear. "But I'm so much better at being bad," he murmured.

They went to several nightspots, drinking and talking, sometimes dancing, until finally Derett brought her to his house. It was only the second time she'd been there—the other occasion being less than romantic—and Loy felt the significance of his choice. When he'd been unable to stay with her even once over the week, claiming his first *New-Sports* articles were overdue, fear had clamped its ugly fist over Loy's heart. But all the worries and doubts she'd suffered evaporated as they nestled together on the plump cushions of one of his rust sofas, drinking champagne and conversing comfortably between sips.

She shifted, kicking her black heels from her feet and tucking them up beneath her. She reached for her glass and hoisted it to him. "Congratulations again, Derett."

His gaze lowered from her eyes to her lips as she drank. A slow curve crept over his mouth. "I'm beginning to think, my sweet, that these continual toasts to me are simply an excuse to quaff more champagne."

Laughing, she shook her head. "You deserve them. Despite your . . . poor aptitude . . . at the first. You've become a good pilot in a relatively brief time. I'm proud of you."

He bent forward to pull off his shoes, then took up his own glass. She studied his profile, examining how the strength of his character was emphasized. It was there in the hard line of his jaw, the firm thrust of his chin. She noticed the jag in his eyebrow and set a fingertip on it. He immediately looked at her.

"How did you get this?" she asked before removing her finger. He caught it and nibbled at it, then grinned.

"I've told you, in a family of seven, you've got to be quick. When I was ten, my brothers Wes and Brad were working together to build a go-cart. They disagreed about it and I walked into their argument. Wes aimed a punch at Brad, who ducked, and hit me, who didn't. He was holding a small wrench, which got me here." He stroked the broken line of his eyebrow.

"What happened?"

He flashed another grin. "It wasn't really much of an injury, but it bled profusely. Brad ran screaming to Mom that Wes had killed me. When it was all over I had several stitches and Wes and Brad no longer had a go-cart. Dad said until they learned how to work together cooperatively, there'd be no cart. And they were grounded a week for scaring my mother."

"Whew. Your father was some disciplinarian."

"Oh, yeah. There were times we thought our old man was an ogre. But we've all turned out okay—happy, well-adjusted, with all the right values. When the time comes, I'll try to be the kind of father he was."

This was a touchy topic. Loy hurriedly turned her attention to the wine. She cleared her throat into the awkward silence, then remarked, "You haven't said what Jeff thought of the first articles you sent out."

"That's because Jeff hasn't said anything beyond his usual editorial grunt to acknowledge them."

"Oh." She searched her mind for something else to say. She plunged in, saying, "I've just about—"

At the same instant Derett started, "You were—"

They both stopped, then laughed. "What were you saying?" asked Loy.

"You go first."

"I was only going to say that I've just about got everything done for tomorrow's barbecue. What were you going to say?"

He leaned closer. His breath nuzzled her cheek. "I was about to tell you that you were the loveliest woman on the town tonight. And that I think we've done more than enough talking."

Her pulse fluttered. "Yes," she breathed, "we have."

He took the glass from her hand and set it on the end table behind him. Then he turned to her and very slowly, very gently, shoved her back into the cushions. He kissed her once lightly, then held himself away from her. With exquisite tenderness he brushed his hands over the length of her bare arms.

Reaching up, Loy laced her fingers through the thick layers of his hair and kissed the curve of his scarred eyebrow, then the hollow above his eye, the bone beside his temple.

Abruptly he caught hold of her hands and held them flat against his chest. "Take me, Loy," he rasped. "Make me yours."

Excitement trembled through her at the hoarse passion in his command. She raced down the row of buttons on his bone-white shirt, fumbling in her haste to undo them. When at last she spread the material wide, she rose up and pressed her lips into the thud of his heart. He groaned as she slid the shirt down his shoulders and from his arms. She threw it in the general vicinity of where his neatly folded suit jacket and tie had been set aside earlier. Splaying her hands over the warmth of his chest, she pushed until he lay prone beneath her.

Derett removed the pins from her hair, spilling strand after strand over his hands. When the last pin slid from her hair, Loy lifted her head and shook it from side to side. Her hair flew out in a flaxen fan, then drifted over her shoulders to caress his bared flesh.

Smiling seductively, Loy slipped down, dropping feverish little kisses from Derett's chin to his belly. Her touch was tantalizingly brief, lingering just long enough to heat his skin with the taste of her lips, the flick of her tongue. Her fingers danced alongside her lips, delicately skipping from rib to rib to rib. She heard his breath come in short, sharp rasps and rose above him, laughing breathlessly.

He captured one crinkly strand of her hair and tugged. "You tease," he half-laughed, half-moaned.

"Two can play the game," she whispered back, her voice low and quivering with desire.

"And two can win," he returned. He caressed her neck, then loosened the clasp of her halter top. As the crepe cascaded to her waist, the amusement vanished from his darkened eyes.

Loy sat motionless, watching him devour her breasts with his heavy-lidded gaze. He cupped them in his palms and she gasped with pleasure.

"Do you want this?" he whispered huskily.

"Yes, yes," she breathed.

"Do you want . . . me?"

For reply, she rose and let the dress slither to the floor. She stepped out of her stockings and panties, then bent and finished undressing him. When his clothes joined hers in a mound on the carpet, she again straddled him. "Yes," she said then.

He did not embrace her, but lay supine, staring up at her. Her heart began to thump painfully, for mingled with the love and desire she saw a thread of sadness in his eyes.

"Do you love me?" he asked finally.

She dropped her lashes to veil the bleakness she felt. "Yes," she admitted. Her voice was paper-thin.

As the silence between them expanded so did her fear. She did not understand what was happening. She'd confessed her love and still he said nothing, did nothing. She could not find the courage to look at him. Then suddenly he was touching her, teasing her nipples with his fingertips, and she forgot the fear in her need to be one with him.

They fused together in a burst of passion. But even as they rode together on the journey to ecstasy, Loy sensed something was wrong. His lips took hers intensely, yet withheld depth. His hands caressed her fervently, but did not yield warmth. His skin melted against hers, but not quite into one. His muscles stretched as he moved with her, but somehow the rhythm was not in sync.

Tremors of doubt overwhelmed quivers of desire. Had he begun to tire of her so soon? Was his love for her a little

138

less today than it had been yesterday? Would it be still less tomorrow?

She cried out his name and it was more than a release. It was a plea. Her cry was lost in the urgent intensity of her rapture and with it, her fleeting doubts. This was all that mattered, this blending of her joy with his.

The moment of tumult passed and Loy's tensed muscles relaxed. She sagged, about to slide down into the comfort of Derett's arms, when she found herself falling, arms flailing, to the floor. Derett tumbled from the plump cushions to land half-on, half-beside her. She grunted at the impact and then, seeing the shock she was feeling clearly imprinted on his face, burst into laughter. After a dazed moment, he joined in.

"Remind me never to go horseback riding with you," murmured Derett as he rolled completely atop her.

"Oh? Why not?" she asked between giggling gasps.

"You can't keep a good seat," he responded. He smothered her indignant objection with a hearty kiss. "But—" he added with another, "a few more lessons—" and another, "and you could be quite an equestrienne."

She blew her bubbles of laughter into his mouth. He retaliated by deepening his kiss, probing and insisting until Loy's laughter retreated before a resurgence of arousal. When he began kissing a line from her mouth to her ear, she suggested unsteadily, "Perhaps we should go upstairs . . . to the safety of your bed. God knows we need . . . safety."

He flicked his tongue over the diamond drop, letting it bob against his lips. "True. We are a dangerous duo. Do you think we need a warning label?"

Rubbing her hands over his back from his hips to his shoulders, she husked, "I think we need a bed."

For just a fraction longer, his jawbone pressed into the soft curve of her cheek. Then he pulled away. "I think we need to get dressed and go home."

"Here will do as well . . . and it won't take us as long

to get upstairs." Her teasing smile wavered, then waned as he refused to meet her gaze. He stood and the pure physical beauty of him shone before her.

"It's time I took you home," he said tonelessly.

For several seconds Loy was too stunned to move. It was as if he'd taken all the sparkle out of her champagne. She tried to summon up a laugh. It sounded brittle. "What's wrong? Got a girl stashed away up there you don't want me to find out about?"

"If I don't get you home, Jeeves will worry." He stretched out a hand to help her up.

She didn't respond to the jest and she didn't take the hand. She sat upright and stared at him. "I don't need to go home. We could stay the night here."

Their eyes held for an agonizing heartbeat. Derett turned away and began gathering up his clothes. "I've made it a policy not to have lady friends stay over."

His light tone didn't soften the insult. The color drained completely from Loy's face, leaving her freckles standing out in vivid highlight. "What did you say?" she asked numbly.

"Come on, honey," he coaxed, again putting out his hand.

She eschewed his help, scrambling to her feet on her own. Feeling like a zombie, she got dressed. She couldn't even feel her heart beating; she wondered dully if maybe it had stopped and she was already as dead as she felt. When she fumbled at the clasp of her dress, Derett came up behind her and brushed her hands away to fix it himself.

"I didn't mean that the way it came out, Loy."

She didn't answer him. It didn't matter how he'd meant it to sound. What mattered was that he'd said it at all. As soon as she felt his hands rise from her neck, she tried to step away. He held her by the shoulders and spun her around.

"Okay," he said through tight lips, "maybe I did mean

that just the way it came out. But you're the one who set the standards of our affair, Loy. You've chosen to be my 'friend' "—his lips twisted as he said it—"and not my wife. I want you in my bed, but permanently, as my wife."

"I think that's a rather hypocritical attitude," she said stiffly. "You've come to my bed often enough."

"Your bed, my bed! Damn it, that's the problem! It should be *our* bed!" He stopped, audibly grinding his teeth. "Marry me."

It wasn't a proposal, it was a terse command issued on a sharp bite. Loy ignored it—and the shrieking pain she felt inside. She picked up her evening bag and asked in a voice of surprising calm, "Shall we leave?"

From the expression on his face, leaving appeared to be the last thing Derett wanted to do. She thought remotely that he had the look of a man about to hit someone. She wondered if it would be she. But then he pivoted, grabbed his jacket from the other sofa, and barked, "Let's go."

The ride from Brookside to Olathe was long and unpleasantly silent. As the heat of her anger dissipated, Loy began to wonder if she hadn't been wrong to take such quick offense. After all, she *had* been the one to demand they keep their relationship on an affair basis—the only time Derett had suggested moving in together, she'd told him no, flatly and unequivocally. The more she thought about it, the worse Loy felt. Derett wasn't the kind of person to say something to deliberately hurt someone.

Still, she had been hurt. It depressed her to think he would keep something, anything, from her. And what did that make her? Just as hypocritical as she'd accused him of being. Wasn't it hypocritical of her to want total commitment from him without being willing to return it?

She cast a sidelong glance at his set jaw. She could see the muscle pull along his cheek and knew he was terribly angry. She looked back out at the sapphire sky blanketing the world beyond the silhouetted rooftops and wished she knew how to erase the ugliness that had passed between them.

When they drove up to her house, he left the car running. An occasional muffled crack of fireworks resounded through the stultifying heat of the night. She put her hand on the door, took a deep breath, and asked, "Would you like to come in?"

He looked at her then, but his expression was shaded by the night. His voice, however, was numbingly chill. "I don't think so. I'll see you tomorrow at the barbecue."

"Okay." She waited a moment more, hoping for something to smooth out this new wrinkle in their relationship. Finally she opened the door and got out. "Good night."

He drove away and she let herself in.

CHAPTER TEN

A fly buzzed past Loy's nose. She whisked it away with an irritated wave of her hand. Heat clustered the short ends of her hair together on her nape; she was glad she'd braided her long hair away from her neck. The slight evening breeze stirred the fluted edges of her silk turquoise blouse but failed to cool her. The warmth sticking to her skin had, she feared, little to do with the setting sun or humid air. It had to do with the steady progression of her evening from bad to worse.

As she thumped the ketchup and mustard bottles onto the picnic table, her mother added mayonnaise and a stack of paper plates. Esther stood back and surveyed the food spread over the redwood. With a click of her tongue and a shake of her gray bob she rearranged a Jell-O salad and a plastic bowl of baked beans, then sighed happily. "Ummm, will you look at that cake? Jackie's got a real flair for baking," she said, admiring a tier of chocolate.

Loy nodded and glanced over the table. Despite the fact that she'd told everyone not to worry about bringing anything, everyone had come bearing cakes and salads, chips and beans. The table was so burdened with food, it was almost sagging in the middle. A reverberating whack followed by a gleeful shout caught her attention and she looked up to see the croquet players congratulating Lisle on a terrific shot. She'd just knocked Bill's ball into the flower bed lining the fence. The fact that everyone else seemed to be having a grand old time rubbed against Loy's fraying temper. She turned to her mother and forced a false brightness to show.

"Well, Mom, I'd say that about does it, wouldn't you?"

"Yes, I'd say it does. Just get everyone something to drink and tell that chef of yours to dish up."

Loy ground her teeth at the coy look that accompanied this reference to the man flipping steaks at the gas grill. She thought if she had to endure one more sly glance, one more knowing smile, she would scream. Hurrying toward the house, she hoped to cross the patio without being stopped. It was, of course, a vain hope.

As she passed by the gas grill, Derett stepped adroitly into her path and grinned. "Darling, you'll have to settle a small disagreement for us. Keith here labors under the belief that you like your steaks rare, but I've assured him you prefer them medium well."

It occurred to her that it was too bad murder was a crime. The two men had cheerfully battled over her all evening and nothing she could say or do seemed to impress upon them that she was not a prize in a verbal shooting match. This, however, was going too far. She'd always had rare steaks to please Keith, who insisted they were better for you that way. She did like them closer to burnt, but she hated to give Derett still another small victory to gloat over.

She glanced at where Keith sprawled over the chaise longue, his brawny muscles straining against the confines of his blue jersey as he rested his head on his hands. A flash of orange blazoned the front of his jersey, inscribed COM-ETS, so Loy deduced soccer was his game this year. She gritted her teeth at his off-key whistling and somehow managed to shape her grimace into a smile. "Actually I prefer my steaks medium rare."

She let the smile slip off her face as she fled into the solitude of the kitchen. It would be a long time, she vowed with a heavy sigh, before she let that man back into her house.

If Loy had been asked just then which man she meant, she'd have been hard put to answer. She was exceedingly angry at the three men who mattered most to her.

It had begun with Keith. As he and Jackie arrived he looked over the front of the house and greeted Loy by saying, "Hey, babe, this place needs a paint job."

"Yes, I know, Keith, but—"

"Well, don't you worry about it, baby. I know a guy who does great work. I'll give him a ring and get it taken care of."

"But, Keith, the carpets need to be replaced and I—"

"Now, doll, you gotta look at this as an investment. You gotta take care of the upkeep in case you ever wanna sell." He'd given her the same patient, I-know-what's-best-for-you-babe smile that he'd given her during their marriage and Loy had clamped her lips tightly together. "If you're worried about the bucks, I'll see what I can do, okay? Now, smile for me, babe, and let me know you're not mad."

How often had she heard that? As she had countless times before, Loy gave in and smiled for him. It hadn't seemed worth starting a scene over, but it had infuriated her just the same.

Then Gary—sweet, solid, reliable Gary—had tossed another log onto the smoldering fire of her ill-humor. He came with a date—a tall, chunky girl whose dark hair and open features could be called more pleasing than pretty. He introduced her to Loy as Tamara, then added, "And this is Loy, Tammie. She's a great pilot and a good boss. But don't listen to anything she has to say about men. She's prejudiced."

They'd all laughed, but Loy had reacted mechanically. She was hurt by his remark, all the more so because of the casual way in which it had been said, as if it were a widely held truism.

It was, however, Derett who'd upset Loy most of all. It was closer to five than to four when he'd arrived and she

145

had nearly given up hope of seeing him at all. But when she did see him, she wished she hadn't.

Everyone was grouped on the patio, still in the process of getting acquainted and catching up on news. Her mother had immediately swept little Keith into her arms, doting on the toddler as if he were indeed her grandson, while Jackie Brenner happily detailed the superior characteristics of her son. Jackie was tiny, with puffs of blond hair and azure blue eyes. She reminded Loy of a china doll, which was precisely how Keith treated her. Loy joined Lisle on the chaise to watch Becky and Jason romp with Jeeves while their father, Keith, and Bill went directly to the ice chest, pulling out cans of beer and loudly discussing the Royals' pennant chances. Beyond them, Gary stood with his arm lightly about Tammie's waist while joking with Roger and Danny.

Into their midst Derett casually sauntered, a wicked grin curving his lips and a dangerous gleam shining beneath half-lowered lids.

With an ear-splitting whoof, Jeeves plunged forward. Being well acquainted with the impact of his weight, the knot of people standing between Jeeves and the object of his adoration rapidly split apart.

"*Sit!*" commanded Derett, scarcely raising his voice.

The flicker of amusement Loy felt upon seeing mouths drop open was the last she'd felt all evening. It had been erased instantly, for Derett ruffled Jeeves's ears, praised him, then turned and said calmly, "I'd have been here sooner, darling, but I couldn't find my shaver. I must have left it here the other night. Have you seen it in the bathroom?"

Loy was not a prude. She was also certain that every adult present suspected the intimate nature of her relationship with Derett. But it was not something one casually tossed out into conversation. Particularly not in front of one's parents. She cast a frantic glance around. The grill, the chaise longue, the cans of beer, had suddenly assumed

146

consuming interest for everyone. She could feel the heat of her furious flush, but was helpless to prevent it from rising over her face. "No," she spat out. To her intense irritation, it came out as a mere squeak.

"How," demanded Lisle, earning her sister's eternal gratitude, "did you do that? Jeeves doesn't obey a soul!"

Hearing his name, the dog perked his head, then lolloped to the chaise where he set his massive forepaws on Lisle's jean-clad lap. Her orders for him to get down were firmly ignored. In turn, Keith and Gary each bellowed at Jeeves, who merely swiped his tongue over Lisle's thrusting hands.

"Down, boy," said Derett sternly but not loudly.

Reluctantly Jeeves removed himself from Lisle's lap. As a collective mass of disbelieving admiration spilled over Derett, Loy gathered the rest of her composure together and stood. She got only as far as the glass doors.

"Do you need help, honey?" Derett queried as he materialized at her elbow.

"No, thank you," she replied in barely civil tones. "I'm just getting the steaks."

"Then I'll definitely help you," he returned.

Whether it was Keith's old protective instinct or a lingering, habitual jealousy from their married years, Loy didn't know. But he suddenly appeared at her other elbow, staring at Derett while assuring her on a slow rumble, "Hey, don't worry about the steaks, doll. I'm gonna take care of 'em."

"That's not necessary—" she tried.

"No problem," he cut in. "I know my way around this grill like the back of my hand. Of course I'm gonna do the steaks."

Derett had done no more than smile at Keith. Then he pressed the flat of his palm against her back and nudged her into the kitchen. Keith had not followed. It was, she thought now as she slammed a pitcher of iced tea onto a tray, Keith's worst offense of the night!

147

Another, smaller pitcher of milk and several empty glasses were added to the tray, then lemon slices, sugar and spoons. The low murmuring of voices floated in from the patio, but Loy didn't pay any attention. She was remembering how she'd whirled on Derett, glaring at him in the garish kitchen light.

"How dare you!" she hissed. "Saying such things, acting as if—as if—" she sputtered into speechless rage.

His split eyebrow jagged upward. "As if we're lovers?"

She focused her gaze on the middle of his fire-red T-shirt and said irrationally, "In front of my parents! How could you?"

"I thought it's what you wanted. I thought you wanted us to act like lovers."

"You thought no such thing," she muttered. She meant to have this out with him, but she couldn't, not just yet. She couldn't tell him what she thought until she could shoo all these people out of her house. Taking elaborate care not to touch him, she moved beyond Derett to take the platter of steaks from the refrigerator. When she left the kitchen, he was beside her with the spatula and turning fork in his hands.

From then on, she'd only spoken to him when forced to for appearance's sake. He, on the other hand, had missed no opportunity to address her with a soft, rustling intimacy that left no doubt at all about the nature of their relationship. She had seen the speculation in the eyes that glanced from her to him; she'd endured the heavy-handed manner in which everyone else avoided saying anything to her while giving her those very looks. The impotency of her fury seemed to strangle her.

Picking up the tray, she took a deep breath to compose herself. Once she stepped through the patio doors, the aromatic sizzle of steaks, the childish shrieks and playful barking, the multiple babble of conversations, helped soothe her. She paused and cast a quick glance around. Fading sunlight filtered through the trees, checkering the

148

yard. The croquet game had ended, and discarded mallets lay in a heap beside the cedar fence. All legs and flaming curls, eight-year-old Becky chased after Jeeves while her shorter, stouter brother stumbled along behind. Nearly everyone else had congregated by the picnic table. Her gaze finally darted to the grill where Derett stood alone. Their eyes met. She took pleasure in letting hers skate disdainfully on.

"Chow time, everybody," she called out as she strode toward the table. At once people began taking plates and finding places to sit. A small card table had been set up for the children and Loy set the milk on it, then put the tea in the center of the picnic table. As she did so, Derett came up behind her with a tower of steaks upon a platter.

"Help yourselves," he said easily, setting the platter down. He slid into place, then patted the empty space beside him. Loy held back. With a smile that to her appeared menacing, he again tapped the wood of the bench. "Sit down, darling."

It was said in the same firm tone he used on Jeeves. Loy sat. What little appetite she'd had vanished. Food magically appeared on her plate, but she found she couldn't eat it. Amid the chatter and chuckles ringing loudly she fixed a smile on her face and counted each interminable minute that crawled by.

"Sweetheart, you're not eating," Derett pointed out.

She picked up her fork. It nearly fell from her fingers when she felt the pressure of his thigh rubbing against hers beneath the table. Through the denim of his faded jeans and the silk of her turquoise slacks, his skin seared hers. She inched her leg away. His followed.

Into one of the silences that inevitably occur at a large gathering, Derett's soft voice suddenly echoed. "By the way, darling, we haven't decided where we'll stay when we go up to Iowa. When we make our reservations we have to be sure to request a king-size bed."

The pause that followed seemed to last a lifetime. Then

abruptly everyone else was speaking at once. Loy tried to keep her smile in place. It wasn't easy. She'd never felt less like smiling in her life. She thought longingly of peppering his steak with arsenic. When she was certain that the conversation surrounding her was no longer forced, she surreptitiously lowered her hand and jabbed his thigh with her fork.

His leg jerked. When the retaliation she expected did not come, she shot a sidelong glance at him. He stopped her breath with a dazzling smile that deepened his dimples. She quickly looked away. Somehow she endeavored to swallow most of the untasted food, to issue comments in a remarkably level voice, even to laugh when everyone else did. She strove not to look at Derett again, but she was violently aware of him beside her. The heat of his body, the brush of his thigh against hers, the flexure of his muscles as he ate, all made it impossible for her to pretend, as she yearned to do, that he wasn't there.

As soon as she noticed the majority of her guests appeared to be finished eating, she stood and began clearing the dishes. She firmly refused all offers of help, insisting they all relax and digest the meal. Lifting a tray piled high with bowls and bottles, she walked to the house. Once in the kitchen she moved automatically, pulling out plastic garbage bags and aluminum foil. She emptied the tray, set a bag on it and turned. The tray tilted and the plastic slithered off.

"Loy, we need to talk," said Derett.

Panic reared up. She had a lot to say to him all right, but she couldn't go through it now and still face her guests. Her knuckles tightened around the edge of the tray. "No," she rasped.

He flinched as if she'd struck him. "You may not want to, but you're damn well going to hear me out."

"I—I can't," she stuttered.

"Too bad. You're going to." His hand snaked out to

clench her arm. "I haven't endured your sneers all night simply to be given the brushoff."

She gasped and jerked her arm, trying unsuccessfully to free it from his grasp. Seeing the angry set of his jaw, she realized the futility of fighting him. She thrust her chin up. "I didn't mean I didn't want to talk to you. Believe me, I have a lot I want to say to you! But not now, not with everybody still here. Please, let's just get through the evening first."

He searched her face intently and his grip gradually relaxed. "All right," he said in a reasonable tone that somehow failed to reassure her, "we'll postpone our discussion—for now. But I'm not leaving here until we've had it out." Loy nodded and he released her. "I'll help you clean up."

Knowing it would be useless, she didn't argue. Together they returned to the picnic table and cleared off the remnants of the meal. They worked silently side by side. It was as if, having decided to wait to talk to her, he couldn't address a single comment to her. By the time they headed back to the kitchen, Loy felt like an explosive waiting to be detonated. Everything, it seemed, was to be on *his* terms or not at all! Well, she had terms, too, and she vowed to make them known.

Her face had always been a mirror of her feelings. As soon as they were inside, Derett said tersely, "Stop pouting. You look about as old as Becky with your lip thrust out like that."

"I'm not pouting!" she denied hotly, sucking in her lower lip. "And who are you to tell me what to do?"

"If you'd act your age," he began, when the sliding of the doors stopped him.

Giving their intent faces curious looks, Lisle swayed in between them. "I know you said you didn't want any help, but I don't have much of a choice. It's either dishes with you or volleyball with those maniacs out there. I'm not about to leap between the likes of Keith and Gary to swat at a solid round flying object. So you're stuck with me."

Loy grasped at this with the fervor of a starving trout clamping onto the bait. "Volleyball!" she exclaimed with flagrantly false cheer. "My favorite game! I'll take your place, Lisle, and you can help Derett finish up."

She was out the door before either of them could sputter an objection. Escaping the tension of Derett's anger, however, proved to be only momentary. Throughout the rest of the evening, his gaze followed her everywhere, dwelling on her with a disturbing intensity. The bright red of his T-shirt hovered on the edge of her vision, blurring all other reality. Loy made conversation without knowing what she said and watched her family and friends shoot off fireworks without knowing what she saw. Once when Becky asked "Uncle Derett" to light a sparkler for her, Loy heard and winced. She caught Lisle's meaningful glance and willed herself not to shriek.

One by one, each of her guests at last bid her good night until only silence and Derett remained. She couldn't remember assuring Keith she'd get the painting done, thanking Tammie and her crew for coming, receiving a fond hug from her father. She could not, in fact, remember anything beyond the frantic pump of her heart, the frenzied leap of her nerves as Derett stood behind her. The door finally closed. Stillness descended like a shroud. Loy very slowly turned.

He waited at the top of the short stairway, leaning casually against the wall. She didn't move and after a moment he mocked her with a smile. "I don't bite."

She mustered her courage then and mounted the steps. "Neither do I."

Quirking his brows as she passed him, he murmured, "You have on occasion."

She wouldn't have thought it possible for her pulse to pound any faster. She was wrong. The susurration of his words and the images they provoked accelerated her pulse to a rate that left her dizzy. In the living room she retreated quickly to the safety of the rocking chair, where he could not sit beside her. With a curl of his lip that told her he recognized the tactic for the cowardly evasion it was, Derett took possession of the couch.

The best defense was offense. Keith had said it a million times. Hoping it was true, Loy launched an attack. "Your behavior tonight bordered on crude. Your insinuating remarks were totally uncalled for, particularly in front of my family."

"I didn't tell them anything they didn't already suspect."

"That's no excuse! You deliberately embarrassed me!"

"Are you sure it's not because I spoke in front of Keith that's got you so upset?"

She ignored the grating harshness of his query. "The way you treated him was positively boorish!"

"And the way you treated him was positively slavish."

Loy looked down at the floor. The memory of their first spontaneous burst of passion there flashed before her. She quickly refocused on the leather thong of her sandal. "He was just giving me some friendly advice."

"I see," he clipped, and she knew he didn't see at all.

"He's used to telling me what to do," she explained lamely.

"So you just let him waltz in and take over. Could it be that you would like him back here telling you what to do permanently?"

"No!" she flared, flinging herself out of the chair. It rocked crazily back and forth, creaking slightly. "Keith meant well and I didn't want to cause a scene, that's all. It wouldn't have done any good for me to object anyway. You can't argue with Keith. He just gets a sad-eyed look of hurt and asks you to smile at him."

She stopped and nearly slapped her brow in exasperation. What on earth was happening? How had she ended up defending Keith? She'd been as mad as hell at him for

153

the very things she was now excusing to Derett! She took a breath to start over when Derett came to his feet and sneered at her.

"Is it really just a *smile* he wants from you?"

Her breath came out on an incredulous gasp. "How can you say something like that? Keith's perfectly happy with Jackie! And he knows I wouldn't—"

"Does he? You seemed damned encouraging to me!"

"Oh! You—you—" she spluttered into fuming silence and looked wildly around for something to throw at him. The sound of his rapid, irregular breathing penetrated her consciousness and she glanced back at him. His face was darkly flushed beneath his tan. As she realized he was suffering some severe strain, her own anger seeped away.

"Damn it, Loy!" he burst out. "Why would you marry him and not me? What the hell did he have that I don't?"

"You're jealous," she breathed in a low tone of discovery.

He strode toward her. "All night I've pictured the two of you together and I had to work not to get sick in front of everyone. If he'd called you babe one more time—"

"Would you have flattened him with your spatula?" she interrupted with an airiness that disguised the depth of her feelings. Wanting to lighten the tension, she offered him a wavering smile. "Or speared him with your fork?"

He stared down at her, his gaze intently searching her face. He fixed on her quivering lips and slowly expelled his rage on a long sigh. "Definitely the spatula. I'm not as adept at fork-spearing as you."

"I wondered at the time how I was going to explain giving you first aid for tine punctures," she said on a nervous giggle.

"And I thought you wanted me to bleed to death." He reached out and traced the curve of her lips with his fingertip.

"It's what you deserved," she said huskily.

"You deserved to be beaten . . ."

Her mouth parted to protest. He swiftly took advantage of the unintended invitation. His kiss held an urgent command. Even as her desire rose up to match his, Loy resisted the surrender his lips demanded. For the past two months her emotions had been wobbling on a seesaw; she desperately needed stability in order to sort them out. She made herself pull free of the intoxication of his kiss. Peering up at him through her lowered lashes, she softly smiled.

"I thought you wanted to *talk*," she teased.

"All I've wanted all night was to be alone like this with you. I was going crazy. I thought I'd have to sic Jeeves on everyone to get them all out of here."

"You know you stunned everybody by making Jeeves obey you. I've never seen so many gaping mouths outside of a fishbowl. Keith was especially impressed. Do you know what he said?" She deepened her voice and swaggered. "Listen, doll, that's some man. You take my advice, babe, and keep a hold of this one."

Derett tugged her back against the solidity of his chest. "Maybe I've misjudged that guy. You should listen to him after all."

She blew a kiss over his ear. "Maybe I will."

His arms constricted about her. He pressed his lips in her hair and groaned. "We can't continue this way. I was sick with fury last night and eaten up with jealousy tonight. I've been behaving like a fool."

A ball of lead settled in her stomach. She feared what was coming and tried to head it off. "Derett, let's just—"

"We've got to get married," he broke in.

She stiffened. He must have felt it, for his arms fell away from her. She backed up a step, then saw his earlier angry pain returning and wished she'd taken two.

"Well?" he snapped. "Don't you have anything to say? You know we can't keep going on like this!"

"I—I thought you said you'd be patient."

"I have been. As patient as I can be."

155

"A month is not what I'd call being patient."

"Five weeks," he corrected her. Her braid flared outward as she shook her head. He reached out and caught hold of it. "I love you. You love me. That usually adds up to wedding bells."

The stricken look she sent him obviously scored a direct hit. He dropped her braid as if it burnt him to touch it. She wheeled and walked to the plant stand. With her back to him, she fingered a tall, upright blade of her mother-in-law tongue and begged softly, "Derett, please don't press me. I'm not ready—"

"Will you ever be? Or is this a line to keep me hanging on?"

The vicious sharpness of his words surprised her. She glanced over her shoulder and winced from the cold fury she saw. Lowering her gaze to the hoya on the second shelf, she mumbled, "I don't know."

"What don't you know? You don't know how I feel? Let me tell you." He came to her in a single swift stride and spun her roughly around. "I feel like a privileged guest who's allowed to stay the night a few times a week. I'm allowed to share your bed, but not your heart. If you've got one, which I'm beginning to doubt. Who's got your heart, Loy? Keith? Stan?"

She shook her head, unable to speak. This savagely biting man was not the Derett she knew; she had no idea how to react to the barely restrained fury he leased on her.

He gave her a shake. "I don't want this for us, Loy. I've tried to show you in every way I know how that we fit together, that my love for you is the enduring kind."

"You think that now, but when you're actually tied down to me you may come to feel differently." Her head was bent, her words scarcely audible.

"What can I do to reassure you? I'll sign in blood if that's what you want!"

Still Loy could not speak. Though she'd known this confrontation was coming, she wasn't prepared for it. For him, everything was so simple. For him, it was black and white—love equaled forever. Loy knew it was neither black nor white, but such fine shadings of gray, they blended into one confusing color. She loved him, but love wasn't a constant she felt she could build her future on. The foundation was too likely to shift, her world to crumble. She needed time to be sure . . .

But Derett wasn't giving her time. He slapped his balled fist into his palm, startling her into looking up at him. "I'm too old to go on chasing rainbows, Loy! I'm not willing to pursue a dead-end relationship. I want a home and family before it's too late for me to have them."

She licked her lips. "Please, I'm not ready for this—"

"I ask you again, will you ever be? You'd like to go on and on, never making a commitment so you can say you'll never get hurt. But damn it, I'm hurting!"

He yanked her into his arms and fiercely thrust his lips over hers. It wasn't a kiss. It was a capture. He forced her head back as his tongue seized the inner depths of her mouth, rousing her to an acute, aching need. She was drowning in the swirling sensations he stirred within her. The passion between them spiraled until Loy had no thought beyond her hunger for fulfillment. The trembling started in her toes and quivered all the way to her head. She felt him shake with the force of it. Suddenly Derett jerked back, holding her at arm's length. Her pulse throbbed insistently as he studied her with narrowed eyes. When he spoke, the uncompromising austerity of his words seemed to come from some other, more distant world.

"I'll give you a choice. Marry me or forget me."

"What?" she asked, stunned. Her mind was still spinning within the vortex of that raging kiss.

"I said, marry me or forget me. I'm not playing this game any longer. Either marriage or nothing. It's up to you."

She stared in open-mouthed astonishment. The bones of

his face stood starkly out beneath the tawny skin. She saw the fulmination of his fury and her own temper rose up to meet it. He had no right to burden her with such a choice!

"You can't issue an ultimatum like that!" she erupted.

"I just did," he bit back. "You don't want to marry me? Fine! I'll accept that and quit wasting my time with a woman who loves her fears more than she loves me."

"That's not true!"

"Marry me and prove it!"

The sounds of their angry voices bounced off the walls. Outside, Jeeves reacted to the shouting by throwing his body against the glass doors and howling. They ignored him.

"I won't be forced into making that kind of choice!" grated Loy. "I'm not ready for—"

"You! It's always you! What about me? What about what I'm ready for?" He drew back his lips in an ugly snarl. "Don't you ever think of me? My needs? Is that how low I rank with you?"

She went rigid, her spine as stiff as a concrete slab. "If that's what you think of me, if I'm so utterly self-centered, perhaps it's just as well we aren't married!"

The breath he drew in could be heard over the dog's continued yowls. "Is that your decision?" he asked, carefully enunciating each syllable.

She said nothing. The tempest of her abrased emotions roiled wildly within her. She thought if she opened her lips, pure venom would stream out to strike bitterly at them both, so she clamped her mouth tightly shut.

Seconds that seemed like hours ticked by. Loy stared at Derett blindly, not seeing beyond her own anguish. He abruptly pivoted and strode away. At the top of the steps he paused and looked back. "Damn you," he said coldly. Then he exited with a slam of the door that rattled the front windows.

Loy clenched her fists and told herself she was glad, glad, glad! He'd been nothing but aggravation since the first moment she'd seen him. He'd disrupted her routine, unsettled her emotions. He'd been jealous and possessive and demanding. She didn't need him! She didn't want him!

The echo of the slamming door died away. The realization came to her fully then. Crystalline tears tracked silently down her cheeks and her fists slowly unfurled, revealing red crescents dug deep into each palm. The truth of it hurt far more than she'd imagined it could.

Derett was gone.

CHAPTER ELEVEN

WELCOME TO IOWA.
A PLACE TO GROW.

Loy scarcely glanced at the sign. She kept her attention fixed, as she had from the outset of the drive, on the road ahead. A vast, clear sky stretched endlessly over gently rolling farmland. Mile after mile advanced, broken only by the continuing passage of old farmhouses with large porches, weathered barns, and green fields speckled with hay rolls and cattle. They crossed Loy's vision in a meaningless blur.

"We're in Iowa," announced Danny from the back seat.

Roger grunted and Gary raised his beer can in acknowledgment. Loy continued to drive.

Shifting restlessly, Dan hunched into the corner, jutting his gangly elbows and knees at varying angles. The disordered scruff of his dark hair fell into his eyes, but didn't hide the frowning glint within them. Loy saw it clearly when she chanced to meet his eyes in the rearview mirror. She thought she saw an accusation and quickly averted her gaze.

"I think I've figured it out," he said suddenly, morosely.

"Yeah? What?" mumbled Roger without much interest.

"We're in the *twilight zone*. We're actually all dead, just corpses taking a boring drive that never ends. We're dead and this is our hell."

A concrete silence dropped heavily. Loy clenched the steering wheel until her hands ached. The pain that had lain twisted in the pit of her stomach uncoiled to strike her. Danny was right. This was hell and she might as well be dead.

Since the night Derett had slammed out of her life, Loy had been trying to convince herself it had been for the best. After all, she knew from bitter experience what emotional damage the entanglement of marriage could cause. She didn't need that. She didn't need Derett Graham.

She was lying and she knew it.

As each long, lonely day crawled by, Loy began to realize that the emotional entanglement of loving was just as agonizing without the marital bond. Though there'd been no property settlements to wrangle over, no drawn-out legalities to get through, the wound cut as deeply. Her heartache throbbed unceasingly. She no longer expected it to go away; her only ambition was to learn how to live with the constant dull pain within her.

Unfortunately the shroud of her unhappiness had mantled everyone around her. The team that had worked together with such cheery efficiency before, now seemed barely able to tolerate one another. Thinking of Danny's acerbic observation, Loy wondered how Derett had been able to integrate himself into her life so thoroughly, so quickly. Right from the start she'd leaned on the certain strength beneath his easy good humor. Right from the start, Roger, Dan, even Gary turned to him with their problems. She should have resented this, but she hadn't. She'd turned to him too. He was the kind of man others naturally relied on. Without him, Loy felt bereft, incomplete. She continually snapped into arguments with Lisle, with her parents, with anyone who came her way. She'd even attempted to argue with Gary, but he, of course, hadn't cooperated. It was as if Derett had been the main thread of her existence and without him her life was unraveling.

The sun struck gold into the amber tassels topping the cornfields they passed. It reminded Loy of Derett's hair when caught by sunlight. Envisioning the warm golden brown of his hair, she also saw the deep green of his eyes, the sensual curve of his mouth, the disconcerting brilliance of his smile.

She focused on a blue sign indicating a rest area and abruptly turned off the interstate. She pulled into the paved parking lot and stopped. Without looking at any of her crew, she opened the door and stated brusquely, "We'll take a brief break." She then hopped out and walked away.

The area was set atop a picturesque crest overlooking a lush valley. Low brick buildings housed restrooms and a tourist information center. Clusters of trees were interspersed with well-mowed lawn and wooden picnic tables. A rustic rail fence ringed the entire area. Loy wandered to the edge, gazing out over the verdant sea of distant tree-topped hills. A brisk wind whipped her long hair into streamers. Birds bickered shrilly, and discordant noises drifted up from the insects hidden in the tall grasses beyond the fence. Listening without hearing, Loy wrapped her arms around herself and tried to stifle the refrain echoing in her mind.

Derett would be in Indianola.

The thought had pounded like a trip-hammer with each rotation of the wheels since leaving Kansas City. She didn't want to admit that a hopeful excitement was growing within her. She didn't want to acknowledge her inner belief that they could somehow settle their differences. And yet . . . he would be in Indianola.

A broad shadow slanted over her. She didn't turn, knowing without needing to look that Gary now stood patiently behind her. Flaxen strands blew golden over the gray of his wavering shadow. She stared at them, waiting.

"Have you found it?" he asked at last.

She slid her eyes in his direction. "Found what?"

162

"The answer you're looking for."

Her gaze dropped, her shoulders quirked. "I don't even know the question," she muttered after a pause.

They gazed at the sun-coated vista. A part of Loy noticed abstractly that certain leaves held a silver sheen where the sun struck them. Another part of her insisted it was time to get moving. Yet another wanted only to turn around and head back home. That was the cowardly part, the part that feared coming face to face with Derett.

"I think you know the question," remarked Gary, still regarding the view. "I also think you know your choices."

"Oh?"

There was more than enough forbidding disdain packed into that single syllable to stop the most ruthless of interfering souls. Gary, however, placidly continued. "You want to know what you should do. You have two choices. Either you love Graham and should go after him—"

Her brittle laugh cut between them.

"Or you don't and should quit brooding about whatever happened between you," he finished calmly. "You've done your best to make yourself and everyone around you miserable. Don't you think it's time you stop wallowing in your misery and do what you feel is right?"

She sucked in a sharp breath, then wheeled sharply to face him. "It's so easy for you to judge! Things may look cut and dried to you, but they're not. It's a tangled web, Gary. How I feel about Derett is knotted up with how I failed at love before. I can't make a relationship work. I'm a jinx at love—do you think I like that?"

"I think you like having an excuse. It frees you of responsibility in a relationship. Whenever you had a problem with Derett, you always had a handy excuse ready. Rather than striving for a solution, you could stand away and say you knew from the start you'd fail."

Shocked and hurt at his brutal assessment, she wordlessly moved away from him. His voice relentlessly followed her.

"Each relationship is unique. You can't judge Derett on the basis of Keith and Stan. Not only is he not like either of them, you're not the same woman who got involved with them. You can hug your fear of love, Loy, but can it keep you warm?"

His quiet question lingered in the air long after his shadow faded away. She told herself he was wrong! He didn't understand. He didn't know what torments she'd gone through. She felt hurt because she'd thought Gary was her friend. She told herself she didn't care. But as she turned toward the Scout, her ears rang with a painful chant.

A woman who loves her fears more than she loves me. You can hug your fear, fear, fear.

She halted in mid-step. Fear. She'd always been afraid, she saw that now. With stunned clarity Loy saw her marriage to Stan Herndon for the escape it had been. She realized she'd always feared not living up to Lisle—feminine, seductive Lisle who had boys lining up for dates even in junior high. Lisle had excelled in drama classes; Loy, who would have preferred drama, doggedly suffered through three years of art to avoid the inevitable comparison. It had nothing to do with her love and admiration for her sister. It simply had to do with Loy's insecurity, her fear of not being quite as good, quite as attractive. When Lisle went on to striking social and scholastic success in college, Loy evaded the entire matter by marrying Stan.

When faced with the truth of her mistake, Loy had raced into the protection offered by Keith. She hadn't stopped to examine what she really wanted, what she could handle on her own. She'd dreaded having her failed marriage compared to Lisle's happy union with Bill and had grabbed the security of Keith. It had taken her years to admit the enormity of that second mistake, but after accepting it, Loy feared nothing more than making a third, even bigger mistake.

By the time she climbed into the driver's seat, Loy no

longer faulted Gary for speaking the truth as he saw it. He had done so because he was her friend and he cared about her. By doing so, he'd given her new insight into her past mistakes. She leaned over and set her hand on the massive width of his thigh.

"Thanks," she whispered.

He grinned. "Think we'll make it in time for the corn-eating contest?"

"Not if we don't get moving." She straightened and started the engine. Indianola was just over an hour away.

Sunshine glimmered like pools of water over the hot pavement. A colorful splash of T-shirts hung at the front of the wooden booth. Loy paused to study the array.

"Why don't you guys pick one out? My treat," she said, gesturing to Roger and Danny. Things were on the upswing since her conversation with Gary the day before. She knew he was right. It was time for her to stop wallowing in self-pity, time for her to stop making everyone else pay for her own mistakes. While the three men had gone to the contest and the square dance afterward, Loy spent the previous evening in her motel room, analyzing herself, how she'd been acting, what she wanted. She was pretty certain now that she had the answers.

She'd been acting like a fool and she wanted Derett Graham.

She had no clear idea what she was going to do about Derett, but she fully intended to stop being the ill-tempered fool with everyone else. Knowing she'd been especially hard on the Perren brothers, she now attempted to make up for it. She'd taken both of them up with her on the morning's pleasure flight and found the old rapport easily reestablished. As the boys began pawing through the display of shirts, all decorated with showy ballooning logos, she stepped back from the crowd to wait.

The broad, flat clip pinning her hair back had become loosened and Loy busied herself with tugging ornery

165

strands back into place. The peacock green of the plastic clip matched that of her short-sleeved cotton top. It was a warm afternoon, even the breeze was hot, and she was glad she'd chosen to wear the lightweight top and cuffed denim shorts. Anything else and she'd be sweltering.

Within the sun's heated lance, a sudden chill crept over her. The back of her neck prickled with alarm. She shivered. A continual tide of people flowed up and down the row of concessionaires and information booths. A large crowd milled about the post office van parked midway down the paved lot. Loy frowned as she glanced around. Goose bumps tingled as they rose on her skin. She recognized the feeling in the same instant she saw him.

He stood on E Street, a stiff figure in the midst of a shifting panorama. He wore an unadorned black T-shirt and faded jeans, yet exuded the special aura of class that had always made him stand out from a crowd. He looked as lean and fit as Loy remembered and his hair still held the muted warmth of sun on sand. But his expression held no warmth at all. Even as her elation at seeing him swelled up, he raked her with a disdainful gaze, then spun and disappeared into the changing pattern of people.

She didn't take time to think, she simply acted. "Here," she said, shoving her purse into Roger's startled hands. She tore down the lot and onto the street, weaving through people, pushing where she had to. There was no plan, no rehearsed speech for her to concentrate on. She only knew she had to find Derett.

She caught up with him beside a stand filled with brightly colored ceramic balloons of all descriptions. When she grasped his arm, he pivoted sharply. His surprise at seeing her was evident in the sudden jerk of his brows. She suspected he hadn't thought she would come after him, and for some odd reason, this doused the excitement she'd been feeling. A sense of doom began to crawl up her spine.

"Uh, hello," she said slowly.

He didn't respond. He stared down at her hand resting

166

on his bare arm. Feeling uncomfortable, she lifted it away. He looked at her then and Loy nearly fled. His eyes had the hard glaze of chips of green glass. His jaw was austerely set and his narrow lips were drawn to a nearly invisible line. He was utterly unapproachable. She cleared her throat.

"H-how are you?"

"Fine," he answered curtly. "And you?"

"Fine." She glanced away from the lack of welcome in his eyes. She noted distantly that the camera strap slung over his shoulder was new. The continuing silence was more stilted than their brief conversation. She licked her lips. "I—I'm glad to see you made it here," she barely got out.

Face and voice remained harsh. "Are you? Why?"

The breeze sang in the windchimes hanging from the stand beside them. She flicked her eyes over him, suffering at the set coldness of his expression, then settled them on the ceramic chimes. "Well, I thought—that is, I hoped—"

"You hoped to play me for a fool again? Watch me dance to your tune again? Sorry, lady, this fool's through dancing."

She was taken aback by the grating vehemence of his anger. "No!" she said quickly, nervously. "No, I just thought we might still be, uh, friends."

His hard laugh held no hint of humor. "Were we ever friends?" he asked in a nasty tone.

If the slightest hope that they could be reconciled had still beat within her, it now died, frozen from the icy blast of that question. Grief suffocated her. She wanted to cling to him, to weep, to beg, do anything to lessen the agonizing ache coursing with the beat of her blood. Instead, a steely pride stiffened her stance, prodded her into facing him directly. "No, I guess we never were," she said flatly.

"On the other hand," he drawled while surveying each curve of her body with open insolence, "we were a pretty dynamic duo in bed." He drew a fingertip over her breast,

167

lazily skimming the nipple hardening beneath the thin material. His touch was warmly intimate. His gaze stayed coldly contemptuous. "I might have time for a roll or two. What motel are you staying in?"

Her gasp was torn from her. Then she was running, blindly and without purpose. She stumbled past trees and shrubs, past buildings and cars, perilously crossing unseen traffic. She collapsed at the edge of a football field, sagging to the grass and hugging her aching sides as she sucked painfully for air.

She had believed Derett incapable of trying to deliberately hurt someone. She'd been wrong. What he had said just then had been intended solely to hurt. It had, badly. She wished she could call upon anger, dislike, any emotion at all, to shield her from the pain. But she'd never been able to stay mad at Derett. How could she dislike the man she loved?

When her clouded vision began to clear, she glanced behind her. The lot was empty. He hadn't come after her. Not that she'd expected him to, not after that ugly exchange. He'd made it patently clear that he no longer held the least feeling for her. If he had ever really loved her, his feelings now amounted to a mere pile of cremated ashes.

Well, what did you expect, McDaniel? To find him carrying the torch despite your rejection? Men only did that in bad movies. Love wasn't something that existed on its own. It had to be nurtured, cared for tenderly, in order to survive. Abuse love and it withered like a plant never watered.

Pulling up clumps of grass and letting the blades trickle through her fingers, she gazed at the main campus of Simpson College. She decided not to look for the guys until the pilot's meeting later that afternoon. She wondered if she'd see him there. Her body trembled at the mere thought of it.

Thank God he wouldn't be competing. He had gotten his license and joined the Balloon Federation of America, but Loy knew he hadn't competed in the three sanctioned balloon races required by mid-June, nor had he logged fifty hours of flight time as pilot-in-command. He was here as a non-competitor, which meant their schedules would be completely different. With luck and care she'd get through the week without again suffering an encounter with him. Most likely he'd be just as anxious to avoid her, so she really didn't have anything to worry about.

So why, asked the nagging voice that wouldn't leave her alone, *are you still shaking?*

A motley assortment of people gathered at the Pote Theatre that afternoon. Ballooning seemed to attract those given to developing outrageous personas; Loy had often thought she was a misfit among the flamboyancy. She felt like that again today, but she didn't think it really had anything at all to do with ballooning. Sitting beside Gary in a comfortably padded theater seat, she nodded at a past president of the BFA, a man whose flowing beard and snowy hair reminded her of Santa Claus. Roger and Dan skipped the meeting to concentrate instead on picking up girls, and the man who took the seat on her left glittered in red satin trimmed with silver. Before her, two men wore beanies with wings at the sides. Loy felt drab, colorless, inanimate by comparison.

The meeting proceeded along the usual lines, stressing the local landowners' rights, the work of the Rural Relations people, rules, safety, and weather. The police chief drew a round of applause and laughter when he ended his short speech with "As far as fixing tickets, we'll talk about that when the time comes."

Loy leaned toward Gary. "Have we gotten any yet?"

A sheepish smile lit his puppy-brown eyes. "One. I was in a no-parking zone on E while we looked for you."

She shrugged and settled back to continue half-listening. Unwillingly her eyes began again to search the room. Scanning the semi-circle of seats, her heart stopped at the sight of soft, sandy hair, then sluggishly returned to work as she realized the short crop was curly and definitely feminine. Her strong reaction filled her with self-loathing. She fought to block out everything but the man speaking below. She was glad she did, for he was giving out the propane schedule. She marked it down on the front of her rules and regulations manual and glanced up.

At the very back of the theater on the right-hand side, Derett leaned against the wall. His bare arms glinted against the dark cloth of his shirt as they crossed over his chest. Though the room was well lit, he melted into a slanting shadow. She couldn't see his face, but she knew without doubt that he was looking at her. She could feel the pierce of his stare.

Somehow she made herself look away. She fixed her gaze on the speaker and didn't move it again for the duration of the meeting. Not one word filtered through to her. The only sound she could hear was the painful clanging of her heart. He was there, so close, yet he might as well have been on the moon. He was beyond her and the sooner she accepted it, the sooner she could get on with life.

For reasons Loy couldn't examine, doing the best she could in the competition suddenly became all-important. Perhaps she sought to vindicate herself in his eyes, to prove she had some worth to someone, somewhere. Loy didn't know and she really didn't care. All she knew was that she was going to make the first cut if it killed her.

She was currently ranked seventy-third in a field of one hundred. After the first four tasks the competitors would be cut to the top fifty. Loy resolved to be one of them. She left the theater with her chin thrust out and her spine stiff.

"Let's find the guys," she said to Gary. "The pilot's briefing is at five at Pickard, which gives us about half an hour."

They found Danny and Roger sitting on the trailer, eating corn dogs. "Did ya see the sky divers?" asked Dan

170

around a mouthful of food. He swallowed and added, "They had square 'chutes, you know, canopies. Looked great. God, I'd love to do that."

"How about getting me one of those instead?" asked Loy, pointing to his corn dog. "And a Coke. Then we'll head on over to Pickard for the five o'clock follies."

As they drove to the park, Loy's adrenaline pumped furiously. She felt electrified. When she strode into the pilot's briefing, however, she received an unexpected jolt. Derett was among the early arrivals waiting for the briefing to begin. She almost walked up to him to demand what he was doing there but a thread of sanity stopped her in time. She didn't care what he did. Nevertheless the event took on an even greater importance. She had to do well. She had to. She didn't ask why.

During the briefing the pilots were provided the most current weather conditions, then informed by the balloonmeister what task they'd be flying. Each competitor was given two Baggies filled with four ounces of corn or grass seed and marked with a three-foot streamer. After about three minutes the knot of pilots fragmented into a footrace back to the cars, each pilot already calculating his flight. Across the flat field, engines roared to life and vehicles sped off into the countryside.

Loy hopped into the passenger seat of the Scout, grabbing her master map and speaking as they pulled away. "It's a two-part task—a CNT on Pickard with a Judge Declared Goal beyond. It's a mandatory pilot solo, so I'll be on my own up there. Winds are southeasterly. I think we should head out toward here." She stabbed a finger at the map. Gary glanced at it, nodded, and turned left out of the park.

A thick, gray ribbon of dust rose from the gravel road as they searched for a launch site at least five miles in the proper wind direction from the target site. Pulling into a driveway, Loy leaped out to ask the landowner if they could use the mowed expanse of his backyard. He cheerfully signed her permission form, then signed for three other balloonists besides. Gary measured wind velocity with an anemometer while the teens dragged the envelope from the trailer and spread it. As if they could sense how much this meant to Loy, they worked together with unaccustomed speed and precision. An official observer watched as they scrambled to get inflated and signaled approval as Loy lifted off.

Later she would remember Derett and wonder how he had done. For now, Loy was unable to think of anything but the task. She checked the altimeter to measure her altitude and the pyrometer to gauge the heat, then swept her gaze over the countryside, visualizing the path she'd take to where the target X would be laid within Pickard Park. Manipulating the burner to gain or lower altitude, she zigzagged through the sky as she aimed for the mark. She paid no attention to the spectrum of balloons surrounding her, nor to the frenzy of chasers below. Her concentration was rewarded. As she descended over the park, she caught a wind pattern that carried her directly over the target. She threw one Baggie at the X, and as she hit the burner to rise, saw it land about eight feet from the center. Elation filled her as she heard the applause from those on the ground.

The target for the second part of the task was easy to spot from the air, but Loy found the wind speed scurrying her beyond it far too quickly. She threw her Baggie in what she hoped was the general direction of the mark and crossed her fingers that it might land somewhere near enough to count. At any rate, the first part of the task was certain to garner her a high ranking.

The thrill of accomplishment rode with her to the completion. She landed with a near-perfect touchdown in a grassy strip ringed by trees and wire fences. Gary and the boys were waiting for her with broad grins and thumbs up. Skipping out of the basket, she began exclaiming, "It was great! Did you see it? I hit about eight feet from the center

172

of the first target and then floated away to the sweet sound of applause. I've never done better, never."

"How about the second?" asked Gary, laughing.

She shrugged unconcernedly. "I didn't get close enough to take proper aim. Without any other weight in the basket the wind just thrust me beyond it before I had a chance. I tossed the Baggie, but heaven only knows where it ended up. But the first one will carry me through, you'll see. I got big points there."

Her enthusiasm was infectious. As they packed up, the crew laughed and joked spiritedly. It was like old times, and for a few minutes Loy knew real happiness. The bubble burst when Roger shielded his eyes against the setting sun's glare and pointed toward the sky. "Isn't that the balloon we rented to Der—er, *NewSports?*" he asked.

She followed the direction of his raised finger to see a globular balloon patterned in yellow and black chevrons skating through the cloudless blue. She didn't even have to look for the identifying number. It was Derett's balloon. Seeing it dampened all her pleasure in her own achievement. "Yes," she replied tersely, looking away. "Let's get going, shall we? I'd like to beat the crowds to the propane station and then get some dinner."

Nothing more was said about the *NewSports* balloon. In fact, nothing more was said at all. Not wanting to, but unable to help herself, Loy fell into a long silence punctuated only by her occasional *tsks* as she wondered just how Derett could be competing. She'd been certain he couldn't have qualified. But apparently he had. Loy resolved to best him.

Once their propane tanks had been refilled, they headed for Crouse Café on Salem Street where Loy assured them they would get the world's best onion rings. It was a typical small-town eatery, with no decor and mismatched cutlery, but the food was terrific and inexpensive. Pilots and crews crowded into the two rooms and the sounds of voices dissecting each maneuver of each flight harmonized into a soothing whole. Loy's good humor gradually returned, especially when Bob Coulter paused at her table to pat her on the back.

"I saw your flight over Pickard and was pretty damn impressed. How'd you do on the second task?"

She gestured toward an empty chair. "Pull up a seat and I'll tell you all about it."

Knowing that next to flying, discussing flights was a balloonist's favorite pastime, they both laughed. He was a slimly built man, stylishly immaculate. Even after a full evening of flying, the khaki slacks he wore were perfectly pressed, the azure polo shirt neatly tucked in at the waist. His brown hair was thinning, but not yet enough to be considered balding, and his face was free of even a hint of stubble. He didn't exhibit the flash or eccentricity so common among balloonists, yet he had a unique aura that made him memorable. Loy had always liked him and she was glad to see him now. Bob grabbed the indicated chair, pulled it up to the end of their booth, and began explaining his strategies for the evening's competition.

A plate of thinly sliced, crisply fried onion rings sat between them. As they talked, Loy urged Bob to eat some. At one point they both reached for a handful at the same time. Their hands collided. Both instantly demurred to the other. Smiling, Bob said, "Let's compromise. You take them, but I get the first bite."

Two months ago, perhaps even two days ago, Loy would have pulled away from the mild flirtation in Bob's suggestion. But she hadn't been able to shake Gary's words from her mind. Even as she felt a twinge of fear, she returned Bob's smile, picked up the rings, and held them for him. He nibbled more of her fingertips than he did of the rings. Seated across from her, Danny and Roger rolled their eyes. Loy saw it and laughed.

"Pardon me for interrupting," said a cold voice that made her choke on her laughter, "but I'd like you to meet someone."

174

Loy snatched her hand away from Bob's lips and dropped the onion rings on the table. In one agonized glance, she saw Derett's arm encircling a willowy, brown-haired woman with a friendly face and pleasant smile. Jealousy stabbed with a sharpness that astounded her. It was a problem she'd never before encountered. She hadn't cared enough about Stan to be jealous of his mistress; she'd been humiliated and hurt, not jealous. Keith had never given her the least cause to feel the deadly sting of that emotion, but even if he had, she doubted it could have hurt like this. This pain pierced the pit of her soul and numbed all other feeling. She longed to cry out, to flee from the torment of it. Instead she forced a cool smile onto her face. "Oh, yes?"

Derett curled his lip derisively, as if he were performing an obligation he detested. He released the woman to step aside for an older, graying man, who bore a perpetually harried air. Not looking at Loy, Derett presented each in turn. "My sister, Maureen, and her husband, Jeff Reynolds, editor of *NewSports*. Loy McDaniel, my pilot instructor."

Quickly wiping her hands on her napkin, Loy reached out and shook hands with each. An unwarranted gush of relief flooded through her. She managed a polite greeting, all the while acutely aware of the unwavering hostility of Derett's gaze. Maureen's smile cooled and Loy wondered why as she turned to Jeff. He, too, had a restraint about him that disturbed her. After acknowledging them both, Loy introduced her crew, then added, "And my friend, Bob Coulter. He's one of the best balloonists in the country."

Ignoring Bob's gracious hello, Derett slanted his lips in a mocking semblance of a smile and began to move on. Loy's tensed muscles started to relax, then knotted with annoyed disbelief as Gary stopped Derett, inquiring, "How did you get into the competition? And how did you do tonight?"

"Jeff arranged it. I'm not being ranked, so I'm not really competing. I'm flying in the tasks and am being given the point scores I would have received were I actually competing. If I don't make the first cut, then I'm out."

"What about tonight?" prodded Roger, earning a fulminating glare from Loy. She just wanted him to *go!* Keeping that smile fixed on her face was making her jaws ache.

With a brief flash of his dimples, Derett shook his head ruefully. "Well, I hit the first target pretty close in—and then rammed my basket on the ground before getting up."

"Oh, no," chorused everyone but Loy. She had no sympathy at all. She was glad. Her smile became more genuine.

"Yeah," confirmed Derett. "An automatic five-hundred-point penalty for touching the ground in the target area." He paused, then queried nonchalantly, "How'd you do?"

It was a general question, addressed to them as a team, but Loy took it personally. Before anyone else could say anything, she said briskly, "Well enough. But we really must be getting back to the motel now. It's after nine and with the next competition scheduled for five thirty tomorrow morning, I think we need to get some rest."

Derett nodded curtly and strolled away without even saying good night. Loy wanted to throw the remaining onion rings at his head, but she politely refrained from doing so. Bob walked with her out to the street before joining his crew for his meal, but she hardly realized he was there. Her mind, her body, her entire being, was drowning in despair. The success of her flight seemed hollow now. All she could think about was Derett's abrupt dismissal. How, she wondered miserably, was she going to get through this week?

CHAPTER TWELVE

"Will you get out of my way?" demanded Loy through clenched teeth. Two infuriating flashes followed, briefly blinding her and blasting her blood pressure to an all-time high.

Derett slowly lowered his camera. With a tight disdain to equal her own, he bit back, "Look, lady, when I'm on an assignment, I don't back off for anyone."

"I don't care about your assignment!"

"Tough," he said, not even glancing at her.

As her vision cleared, Loy unwillingly focused on the long fingers readjusting the camera lens. Unwelcome images of those browned fingers curling over the cream of her breasts rose before her. She blinked, and wished she hadn't. She found herself staring at the low-slung waist of his jeans; the memories *that* evoked were simply too painful to be borne.

"For the last time, Graham," she said in a voice muffled with fury, "quit bothering me."

"For the last time, lady, I don't give ground for anybody when I'm shooting."

He raised his camera and she noted the slight stiffening of his body as he braced to take aim. The fluid beauty of it momentarily mesmerized her. The glare of his flash startled her. She abruptly realized he was again taking snaps of her, with her crew lounging in the background. Raging, Loy spun sharply on her heel and stamped off.

A light gray haze had gradually leached the purpureal

hue of dawn and she had no difficulty seeing her way across the flat field, hedged on both sides by rows of vehicles waiting to roar into action. Pickard Park had again become a parking lot as balloonists waited to launch into this fifth morning of competition. Throngs shifted around a small wooden coffee stall. She passed them by, turning onto the road, heading for the briefing headquarters. With each terse step the crunch of gravel beneath her feet sounded an angry beat. It crackled with the same furious message pounding in her pulse.

She had to get away from Derett.

Her steps slowed, then halted. She realized it would not be easy. She'd tried to avoid him the day before and discovered it wasn't possible. He seemed to have become her shadow. A chill shadow that frosted her blood even as the morning air numbed her skin. She wrapped her arms within her navy sweat shirt tightly around herself, then glanced over her shoulder. He wasn't there.

Instead of the expected surge of relief, an upswelling of dissatisfaction shook her. Once again Derett was making it painfully clear that he'd have found the presence of a rabid dog preferable to hers. He took his pictures, then dismissed her, turning to Gary or the Perrens and joking as easily as he ever had. Loy bit her lip, not feeling the sting of it. The piercing in her heart overwhelmed any other pain she could possibly feel.

This was a nightmare, an absolute nightmare. Seeing him, being near him, was torturing her. Her blood responded to each breath he drew, each movement he made. Seeing the long line of his legs, she remembered the strength of them twined about hers. Seeing sunlight streak over the fine gold hair along his tanned arms, she remembered the glimmer of moonlight threading over them as he held her. Her mind overflowed with visions of all that she had lost.

Why didn't he go?

178

Loy forced herself to walk on, knowing she could have plucked tunes on her tautly stretched nerves.

The week of competition was always hectic, the erratic schedule of early mornings and late nights quickly depleting physical resources. For five days now she'd been up before dawn and not in bed before midnight and it was wearing on her, emotionally as well as physically. The competition was tough, requiring coordination, concentration, and discipline. She'd been far too keyed up to get any rest between times, her nerves leaping like spit on a hot griddle. Though she attributed this solely to the championship, Loy knew in the depths of her heart it had more to do with one obnoxiously persistent photojournalist.

Having more or less knocked himself out of the competition with that first enormous penalty, Derett hadn't made the first cut, but any pleasure Loy might have taken in knowing she bested him was squashed by the thought of his leaving Indianola. For reasons she still didn't want to face, it depressed her to know that once he left, she would never see him again.

But with typical perversity, Derett hadn't left. He'd attached himself to her crew, ignoring her vehement and repeated objections. It was all, he insisted, for the wrap-up of the story. When Loy coldly pointed out that she had fulfilled her obligations to *NewSports,* had been paid for her services and was no longer required to assist him in any way, Derett simply shrugged.

"I can get by without your help, lady."

"Stop calling me that!" she crossly returned.

He merely lifted his shoulders again. "Mostly all I want are action photos. I don't need your approval for that."

Gnawing on her lower lip, she glared at him. She couldn't say, *The mere sight of you disturbs the rhythm of my heartbeat.* Instead, she said pointedly, "This is a competition and I intend to win."

"So? Who's stopping you?" he asked with a scornful curl of his lips.

"Just make sure you don't get in my way" was her parting shot.

"Make sure you don't get in mine" was his.

Since then, each click of his camera echoed mournfully in her heart. She couldn't have said which was worse, the thought of never seeing him again or being forced to see him continually, knowing he couldn't stand the sight of her. She could only hope she had managed to disguise how badly she was suffering.

Reaching the circle of pilots already within the briefing area, she calmed herself with a deep breath. There was no sense in getting herself all worked up. She needed to put Derett out of her mind, to concentrate on this third finalists' competitive task.

And still the angry snap of his shutter release reverberated within her.

A man in a spotlessly white dress suit splashed with a frilled scarlet shirt and snowy bow tie came up beside her. "Why the frown? Something gone wrong this early in the morning? Or have you just seen yesterday's ranking?"

She glanced up quickly and the crease in her brow smoothed away. "Morning, Bob." She eyed him from head to toe, then smiled. "Don't you think your jogging shoes are a bit . . . incongruous?"

He grinned and jauntily tugged the ends of his bow tie. "Classy, huh? But you didn't answer my question. What's wrong?"

"Nothing," she replied quickly. "I'm just anxious, that's all. I never realized that the better you do, the more the pressure builds up. How have you done it all these years?"

Though his eyes seemed to say he didn't accept her reply, he followed her lead and launched into a general discussion of the perils of doing well in competition. More and more balloonists mingled with them and eventually the meeting got under way. After weather reports giving wind direction and speed, the balloonmeister announced

180

the task and the group dispersed into a conflux of stampeding runners.

Dashing up to the Scout, Loy announced tersely, "We're to launch here. It's an Elbow. Let's get going." While her crew scrambled to roll out the envelope, she plodded a possible course on the master map. She saw Derett helping Danny with the balloon, but really didn't feel she could protest. This event was too important. The Elbow was not only one of the most difficult tasks, this was the last task before the final eliminating cut to the top ten competitors.

She leaped up and shucked out of her sweat shirt to reveal a faded pink T-shirt with a baby blue balloon and the legend HOT AIR IS MY BAG across the front. Her adrenaline flowed at full speed as she raced out to help the crew get her aloft.

Excitement pulsated as she worked, her mind focusing on the task ahead. She would have to fly to a spot at least three miles from the field, mark her set-down, then launch again and fly to a second spot, attempting to change course as much as possible. The variance she achieved in the course would be the major factor in her score, a change of 180 degrees being considered perfect.

When an official finally handed her the go-ahead to lift off, Loy hit the blast valve hard and the balloon shot upward. She'd once told Derett that the wind is fickle, like a river flowing over rooftops. This morning the wind-river was a turbulent stream of cross-currents, and as the burner blasted noisily, Loy searched for a strong current to carry her to the right of the park. She found it at a thousand feet and maintained the height until she lowered to drop her first marker over a clear patch of empty field beyond a grouping of farm buildings.

Below, a band of pavement curved around the circumference of the grassy field. Another, narrower strip of gravel bisected it at mid-section. Chase vehicles kicked dust into the air as they whisked in both directions following balloons that were scattered like dandelion seeds over the countryside. Non-competitors had taken off from Simpson Field at the same time the competitors lifted out of Pickard Park and the bluing sky provided a spectacular backdrop for the multitude of colorful teardrops gliding with the dawn.

Having tossed her marker, Loy rose slowly, with short bursts of heat. She caught a current going to the left near ground level, and made her turn in direction. Her heart began to kick happily. The change in her course was abrupt, almost a perfect about-face. She hugged the ground, mentally measuring the distance she had to travel before landing. She looked out over the field, seeing other balloons touching down in the distance. Off to the side she spotted the Scout following along the gravel road. She raised her hand to wave, but it hung limply in mid-air. Her heart plummeted.

Directly in her wind path, wires stretched across the sloping field.

She knew instantly she would either have to cut danger-ously close to the power lines and land beyond them or raise and change direction, ruining her course. Normally Loy would not have risked the power lines, not for any competition. But this wasn't just any competition. It hadn't been from the moment she'd seen Derett Graham amid the shifting crowds on E Street. Without fully under-standing why, Loy had felt compelled to do well. She had to prove herself—if not to him, then perhaps to herself.

She gauged the distance and height to the wires, saw the flat open expanse beyond the lines, and decided to go for it. Her impulsive go-for-it attitude had gotten her into trouble before. And would, she fervently hoped, do so again. For now, she would attempt to rise up at the last possible moment, then land on the other side of the field. She settled her hand on the valve. "No guts, no glory," she whispered hoarsely.

As she hurtled toward the power lines, Loy had to fight

182

the impulse to shut her eyes. But she had no time to indulge in fear. The velocity of the wind had increased steadily throughout her flight; it now gusted strongly, shuttling her over the field and directly at the wires. At the same moment, she hit the valve and partially opened the deflation port. Her heart in her mouth, Loy fixed her gaze upward, watching flames shoot into the puffed fabric while her pulse counted each foot of her ascent. It seemed to her that the balloon took forever to respond to the heated message she sent.

The tension wires were suddenly below her. The wicker narrowly missed scraping the lines. And then she was beyond them.

Before she could breathe a sigh of relief she was flung wildly toward the ground. Since she'd already vented, the wind yanked at the envelope, thrusting her forward without control. She just barely had time to shut off the burner valve before crashing with a massive jolt into the dirt. She was thrown from the basket onto her back. A propane tank bounced free of its mooring in the wicker, rolling just inches past her shoulder. Then it was all over. Although she'd landed without grace, she'd landed safely and right on course.

She lay where she'd fallen, gasping for breath and trying to still the trembling of her limbs. Her mind sang with the knowledge that she'd done it, she'd done it. Finally she sucked in one last gulp of air and pushed to her knees. Looking over her shoulder, she peered through the wind-blown tangles of her hair. She gulped as she realized she couldn't have missed the power lines by more than five feet. Her already weak legs instantly wobbled like jelly. But Loy didn't have to worry about standing. She was jerked roughly upright before she had a chance to try.

"Just what the hell do you think you were doing?" demanded a furious voice. "What were you trying to prove?"

Loy shook her head to clear the fuzz from her still

frightened brain and focused on Derett's angry frown. "I wasn't proving anything," she said weakly.

"Oh, yes, you were!" he countered hotly. "You were proving what a damn-fool idiot you can be! Do you realize how close you came to those wires? You could have been killed!"

His hand pinched her arm where it gripped her; his lashing words stung her. Loy was dimly aware of Gary, Roger, and Danny standing just behind them, of the two other balloons deflated nearby and the crews standing around them, of the official observer hovering by her elbow. The one Derett wasn't clenching. A hot flush of embarrassment ran over her face, washing over her freckles until they could no longer be seen at all.

"But I wasn't, was I?" she asked as steadily as she could.

"Only by a quirk of luck—"

"That wasn't luck! That was skill! I came in at close to a perfect one-eighty turn and—"

"I don't give a damn about the turn!" he cut in. He gave her arm a vicious shake that rattled her to her back teeth. Her flinch only seemed to goad his anger further. "You nearly hit those lines! What kind of a fool are you, taking such a stupid chance? And for what? A goddamned moment of glory?"

In the distance burners whooshed and birds shrilled. The hum and buzz of insects swelled into the silence. Loy looked wildly around at the strangely immobile ring of spectators. Not one person out of fifteen seemed willing to risk Derett's rage in order to rescue her. Even Gary stood well back with his gaze fastened on the toe of his tennis shoes. She glanced back at Derett. A dark stain spread beneath his tan, deepening the austerity of his features. She'd never seen him like this and it frightened her. But it also annoyed her. She didn't understand what he was so furious about.

"Why are you so upset? Nothing happened. I knew what I was doing—"

"Like hell! If you'd known what you were doing, you'd never have gone up with a CB that doesn't work! I can't believe you'd be so damned dumb as to not get that radio fixed. Do you know what we went through trying to reach you, to warn you?"

She slid her gaze past the blazing fury in his eyes. "But nothing happened—" she tried to say again, infusing as much calm into her voice as she could manage. It wasn't easy. Any calm she might have mustered after that hair-raising brush with death withered beneath the terrifying threat in Derett's raging face.

He clenched his jaw and looked ready to do what the power lines hadn't. "The fact that nothing happened is pure luck. What could have happened—"

"But it didn't!" she burst out, her temper erupting at last. "Let me go! I don't understand why you're acting like this! So I came down on a jolt—*you've* touched down as roughly as this."

Instead of letting her go, Derett gave her another shake. "Don't you *ever*"—shake—"take such a *stupid*"—shake —"risk again," he ordered.

With a final, irritated jerk, he at last released her arm. Loy stumbled back, caught herself, and gaped at him in astonishment. Bringing her lips together on a snap, she demanded crossly, "Just what does it matter to you anyway?"

"It matters, you pigheaded fool, because I love you!" roared Derett.

In the brief silence that followed, Loy was certain every person present could hear the shocked thud of her heart. She stared at Derett and struggled not to fall over. Her brain tried to translate what her ears thought they had heard. She'd been so certain he no longer loved her, so certain she'd killed his tenderest feelings for her, so certain she'd lost her chance to love him in return. . . .

185

Ignoring the avidly listening crowd surrounding them, Derett loudly continued. "I love you and I was worried sick about you!"

"Derett, I—"

"You put me through hell sweeping over those lines like that! Of all the stupid, childish tricks—"

"Derett, please, I—"

"Shut up! If you weren't such a stubborn, ornery idiot of a female, you'd stop torturing me and marry me!"

She glared at him. How could he have failed to see the answering love in her eyes? How could he have failed to hear the wild pounding of her heart? Throwing back her disheveled hair, she set her hands on her hips and yelled, "All right, I will!"

He opened his mouth, then closed it and finally opened it again. "You'll what?"

"I'll marry you, and it'll serve you right!" she shouted.

After a short, stunned silence the group around them began clapping and cheering. One man raised a call for action. Derett responded, reaching for her. She felt the warmth of his encircling arms, the solid haven of his muscular chest, and beneath the screech of high-pitched whistles and laughter, she heard the unsteady thump of his heart beating against her own. The erratic rhythm rang in her ears. She bent her head back to tell him this, but her words were stifled by the predatory hunger of his mouth capturing hers. She met the passion of his kiss with the heat of her own. How she had longed for this! How she had missed the wondrous joy of their lips burning together. The last vestige of doubt faded away. This was right. This was where she was meant to be, with Derett.

Someone had uncorked a bottle of the ever-present champagne and suddenly they were being drenched in a fizzling spray. They broke apart in laughter, but Derett kept his arms about her. She gazed up at him, watching rivulets of champagne trace golden trails over the planes of his face. She longed to chase the course of each glisten-

186

ing drop with her tongue, to kiss each away until only the heat of her lips covered his face. The intensity of her desire shook her. She lowered her lashes and murmured breathlessly, "You were right, you know."

He dragged his gaze from his perusal of her figure within his embrace. He spoke slowly, as if he had to concentrate on each word. "I generally am—but what are you talking about?"

Loy swayed closer, whispering huskily. "Bathing in champagne *is* a great way to start a relationship."

A sudden spark of passion shone within his green eyes, glittering with a heat that warmed her. "Great? It's fantastic," he countered.

She nodded in happy agreement and for an instant his hold tightened. Then he let her go and with all the aplomb of a gracious host at a private party, he thanked the balloonists and crews, accepted the remainder of the champagne, and asked Gary to take care of the packing up. Before Loy could remark on the ease with which he'd dispatched them all, he swept her into the back seat of the Scout and folded her into his arms.

"Are you okay?" he asked on a husky note.

"Umm," she nodded. Snuggling closer into his shoulder, she said cheerily, "I've probably got a few bruises here and there. Mostly I just had the wind knocked out of me."

"What about your back?"

"It's okay, really." She shot a twinkling glance at him. "Admit it, I pulled it off. I judged that rise over the lines to a T." She saw his jaw clench at the memory and knew he'd never accept the skill behind her narrow escape. Determined to distract him, she laughed provocatively. "The worst part was the shaking up I got afterward."

He glanced down at her and the tension in him eased. "I was trying to jolt some sense back into you," he said with a self-righteous air. "Must have done the trick, too, or you'd never have said you'd marry me."

She was silent, a little smile dancing over her lips as she

remembered the scene—her yelling and the crowd cheering. She felt the tension come into his arms, heard the ragged edge to his breath. She was about to ask him why, when he suddenly sat her up and held her at arm's length.

"You did mean it, didn't you, Loy? You will marry me?" Without giving her a chance to answer, he scowled and said, "It doesn't matter whether you meant it or not. I'm holding you to it. I've got witnesses—over a dozen— and by God, you're going to marry me."

"Of course I meant it," she countered indignantly. "I always mean what I say."

Relief and love flooded together in his eyes. He leaned forward to press his lips against her damp hair. "If we leave right now for Kansas City, we can be married by the end of the week," he suggested on a low husk.

"But, darling, the competition," she began, only to stop as she saw the opaque glaze she'd come to know and detest in the last week stealing into his eyes. She set her fingertips against the tawny surface of his cheek. She could feel the rigidity of his tension. It was her first test, and if she wanted him, Loy couldn't afford to fail. She let her love glow in her gaze. "Yes, we'll leave now, if you want.".

He searched her eyes. "What about the competition?"

"There's nothing that means as much to me as you do."

Like air rolling out of a balloon, he slowly relaxed. "I guess I can make myself wait, especially as you have a chance to win this thing."

"We could go," she persisted. "I doubt I'll win."

Drawing back, he gazed down at the champagne clinging to her shirt. "You could win a wet T-shirt contest," he said unsteadily.

She glanced down and saw her nipples thrusting against the thin, damp material, dark aureoles beneath the pink. For one moment the old fears returned. Would he tire of her? Cease wanting her, then cease loving her? Her eyes darkened to the shade of a stormy sea. When he reached

188

to pull her back against him, Loy put out her hands to hold him off.

His sudden frown reappeared. "What's wrong?"

"I—" She nervously ran her tongue along her lips. She really didn't want to bring it up. She didn't want to spoil the beauty of having his love. But Loy felt she owed it to him. She loved him. She had to warn him. She pressed her fingers together and forced herself to speak. "Derett, I've got to warn you that I'm a—a bad risk at marriage. I'll try, I really will try, to be a good wife, but I haven't done too well before and—"

"It takes two people to make a marriage work, my sweet," he interrupted softly.

"Yes, but—but you might tire of me. I haven't worn well before—"

"For the last time, quit comparing me to your other husbands. Our marriage won't be like those."

"Yes, but if something goes wrong, I want you to know I won't hold you to it. I'll let you go anytime you think our marriage has failed—"

"Well, don't expect the same courtesy from me," he cut in, a slight glint of humor in his gaze. "I'm not letting you out of our marriage for any reason. We won't fail, Loy. Believe me, I intend to work hard at making ours a success." He let his eyes drop to the outline of her breasts against her T-shirt and added suggestively, "And there's so much to work at . . ."

Framing her face with his hands, he kissed the top of her damp hair, the curve of each eyebrow, the golden fringe of her lashes. He pulled away. When Loy lazily lifted her lids, she saw him studying her with a savage intensity. His gaze met hers and she drew in a sharp breath at the stark desire within his. She still wasn't certain he understood the problem.

"I'm a jinx at love," she moaned unsteadily.

"You're my jinx," he contradicted.

"How do you know—" she started, but he cut her off.

Pressing his fingers into the bones of her face, he tilted her head back and kissed her ruthlessly, feeding upon her lips as a starving man upon a banquet. When Loy had no power to draw a single breath, he drew away and gazed at her. His eyes were dark, but glowing. His mouth had the fullness of passion softening them. His fingers still warmly cradled her head and his breath caressed her skin.

"Don't you know, my lovely jinx," he softly asked, "that the third time is said to be the charm?"

When You Want A Little More Than Romance—

Try A Candlelight Ecstasy!